GO WEST, INSPECTOR GHOTE

GO WEST, INSPECTOR GHOTE

H.R.F. Keating

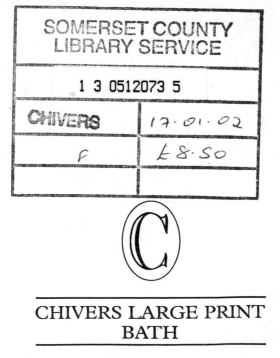

CHIVERS LARGE PRINT
BATH

British Library Cataloguing in Publication Data available

This Large Print edition published by Chivers Press, Bath, 2001.

Published by arrangement with the author.

U.K. Hardcover   ISBN 0 7540 4544 7
U.K. Softcover   ISBN 0 7540 4545 5

Photoset, printed and bound in Great Britain by
Bookcraft, Midsomer Norton, Somerset

GO WEST,
INSPECTOR GHOTE

CHAPTER ONE

The man's office was enormous. Inspector Ghote, at the door, stood stock-still unable for a moment to take a step forward so overwhelming was the effect.

Even its occupant, at whose urgent request he was there, seemed shrunk into insignificance behind his huge, carved table-desk at the far end. Yes, even Mr Ranjee Shahani, the crorepati, the 'magnate' as the English-language newspapers called him, the head of Shahani Enterprises itself, was dwarfed here.

But why had this man, this magnate, requested the presence of a simple inspector of the Bombay CID? And so urgently? And why had it been that nothing could be told him about the reason for the request?

Ghote drew in a breath, still without setting foot on the first of two vast carpets that lay between him and the crorepati's huge table-desk, and the very air he sucked in seemed a different substance from the damp, sullen atmosphere of end-of-monsoon Bombay outside. It was air-conditioned to a chilliness that put him in mind of the snow-crowned Himalayas.

'Mr Shahani? It is Inspector Ghote.'

He wished violently that his voice had

1

sounded less dry in the back of his throat.

The magnate, the crorepati, there at the far end of the huge room, lowered his head in slight acknowledgement.

'Yes,' he said. 'It was Inspector Ghote.'

Was? It was Inspector Ghote? Why, why, 'was' and not 'is'?

'Come, Inspector.'

Ghote plunged on to the carpet in front of him, a softly shining expanse of pale, marked-at-a-touch fawn with mysteriously contorted bluish dragons disporting over it, fetched at some time long past from Ancient China. Dimly, as he advanced, he was aware of the walls of this 25-storey-high paradise, great areas of slatted wooden blinds that turned to cool dimness the harsh sunlight striking at the floor-to-ceiling windows behind. Massive earthenware tubs and fat sagging baskets held richly green plants reaching up on slender trunks to the very top of the airy room or tumbling in lush cascades to its floor.

Behind the gleaming desk with its bulging legs carved into the shape of yet more dragons, sharp-clawed and vigilant now, the small crouched figure of Mr Ranjee Shahani watched him in unbroken silence.

He stepped off the first carpet, on to the second, as big, as pale, as dragon-writhing. He squared his bony shoulders in a sudden access of resolution.

2

But why, oh why, did this have to be the day he had put on his oldest, thinnest shirt, the white one with the wiggly red squares?

And now at last he was in front of the crorepati's desk, that huge glinting rectangle of highly polished wood edged with a wide band of intricate carving, its surface broken only by a gold-tooled leather blotter—but that must be at least five feet long and three wide—a telephone in dully gleaming gold on the right and a paan-box in equally solid gold on the left.

He brought his eyes up to look straight at the crorepati. Framed by his tall, leather-backed, deeply-buttoned chair, Mr Shahani sat unmoving, a well-fleshed bullfrog pensive over which darting, ignorant fly next to snap up.

'Sir?' Ghote said firmly.

'Ah, yes. Yes. Well, I have spoken to my very good friend the Minister for Police Affairs and Cultural Activities, and he told that if I am wanting a CID wallah with thee-four weeks' leave due then it was Inspector Ghote I must ask for.'

Yes, Ghote acknowledged with an inward foreboding. it was true that he had accumulated at least four weeks time off-duty, overdue annual leave, casual leave and leave in lieu of extra days worked. Next week he was due to begin using up a good deal of it. To go with Protima and little Ved, before school began again, to Banaras, most ancient and most holy of

3

all the cities of India.

And now it looked as though that long-awaited trip was about to be cancelled. Influential Mr Ranjee Shahani had asked for a CID man with plenty of free time at his disposal.

Into Ghote's head there flashed contradictory emotions. To be chosen for whatever task it was that this most important person wanted performed: it was a mark of trust, of high trust. To have to perform whatever task it was, it could well prove beyond his powers, beyond anyone's powers, and then . . .

And, another thing, and worse. Banaras. It was not where he himself would have chosen to go to shrug off for a little the burden of combating crime in swarming, heat-oppressed Bombay. Banaras was Protima's choice of place, and she had made it one on which there rested the whole state of their life together. If he was going to reject her long-cherished yearning to step into the waters of Holy Ganges at their holiest point, then, she had declared, she would know finally that their marriage was no longer the union of two souls it had so clearly been in its first months when they had come to love each other. If she did not get to Banaras this time, she had said—well, shouted actually—she would know they were linked only in a dust-dry contract, for him to provide a roof, food and clothes and for her to cook that food, mend and get washed those clothes, order what lay beneath that roof.

Inspector Ghote licked his dry lips.

'Sir—Sir, what is it that I can do for you?' he asked.

The crorepati did not reply immediately. And when he did it was in a slow, thoughtful tone.

'Inspector, what I would say to you is altogether most confidential. Nothing of it is to be spoken to any other person whatsoever. I would not want to have to mention you after to my very, very good friend, the Minister for Police Affairs. Not one word beyond these walls. Ever.'

Ghote let his eyes flick swiftly away to the areas of glass shaded by their smart, slatted blinds and lush green plants. He felt a hot, harsh wind of anger rise up within him at the crudeness of the crorepati's threat. He would have liked to let it sear out.

'Not a word of course, Shahani Sahib,' he made himself murmur discreetly.

'Inspector, I am a poor man.'

Ghote fixed his eyes firmly on the unblemished white paper in the huge leather-tooled blotter at the desk's centre rather than let them stray for even the shortest betraying instant to the gold-plated telephone or the solid gold paan-box.

He waited.

'Inspector,' Ranjee Shahani went on with a

5

long sigh, 'some of the world's goods I have. I have earned and earned them with the labours of my head. But in one thing, Inspector, I am altogether lacking.'

Ghote knew that he was not expected to ask what this one thing was. When Ranjee Shahani was ready to disclose it he would do so.

Abruptly the crorepati put his two pudgy little hands down flat on the unsullied blotting-paper in front of him.

'Inspector, I am a man without sons. Almost I am a man without children. I have one daughter only. One daughter only.'

We are two: we have two. The old family-planning slogan came into Ghote's head. Well, if children were wealth, then Ranjee Shahani was half way there at least. As he himself was with his one son. But why was he being told this tear-jerking film-story tale?

'Two years ago, Inspector,' the crorepati went on, placing every word down as if it was a weighty coin, 'I sent that one daughter of mine, Nirmala by name, to America. For her education, you understand.'

'Yes, sahib.'

Of course anybody of Ranjee Shahani's wealth and influence would want to send their only child to the USA, or at worst to the UK, for final education.

'Inspector, until thee-four weeks ago we were receiving aerogramme letters from Nirmala

6

written each Sunday informing us of the great, great progress she was making at her college. Her college in California, Inspector.'

Ghote realized that he was expected to bring an expression of admiration on to his features at this. California was plainly a particularly special part of America. But where was it? Where? Yes. Yes, that was it. In the far west, as far west as you could go. California.

'And then suddenly, Inspector, nothing. Nothing, nothing. One week missed, two. Three. We are telephoning, telephoning. She had left the college they are saying. Whereabouts unknown.'

Ghote felt a lurch of unstoppable dismay. The crorepati's only daughter missing in America, in California. And he himself must have been summoned here then to be sent to that unknown, distant territory to find her.

'Mr Shahani—' he began.

The crorepati ignored his half-uttered objection.

'What to do, Inspector?' he said. 'What to do? But well I am knowing what to do. *Jaldi, jaldi* a private eye I am hiring. Two hundred and fifty dollars a day plus expenses. That is Rupees two thousand per day, Inspector. Rupees two thousand.'

Ghote, suddenly freed of the prospect of having to conduct an investigation in distant, strange, complicated, unknown California felt a

7

sense of awe invade him. Two thousand rupees a day. In a single day to earn nearly twice as much as he himself brought down in a month. What a marvel of a man, of a detective, such a person must be. And, of course, such a man must have succeeded in locating Ranjee Shahani's missing daughter, though if so, why—

'In two days my private eye had found.'

Ghote let a broad smile come on to his face.

But no matching smile showed on Ranjee Shahani's round, well-fleshed features. Instead, plain to see, a look of smouldering rage was gathering there.

A pudgy fist rose up and beat the unsmirched white blotting-paper.

'She will not come back, Inspector. That man says she is happy-happy where she is. He is a damn fool only.'

A damn fool. On two thousand rupees a day, plus expenses. It could hardly be. But what wealth must Ranjee Shahani have to be able to say that, to be able to think it.

'Do you know where that stupid girl has put herself, Inspector?'

And this time, it was clear, the crorepati did want an answer. But where—where in America? In California?—could the girl have gone?

'She has taken job, sir,' he tried. 'Some job paying Rupees 60,000 p.m.?'

'Inspector, if Nirmala was wanting that much money per month, do you not think I could give

8

and give?'

'Yes, sir. Of course, sir. Easily you could give.'

Ranjee Shahani blew fiercely out between puffed cheeks.

'No,' he said, 'Nirmala has entered an ashram.'

'An ashram, sir? But then she has come back to India? There cannot be any such holy places where you are able to cast off the cares of the world in California.'

'There are such places there, Inspector. There are. I have talked with my friend the Minister and he has talked with his friend in Delhi. External Affairs, Inspector. And they have consulted Consul General in Los Angeles, California. And, Inspector, it seems that in what they are calling the Golden State there are many, many ashrams. And it is in one of these that my Nirmala is being kept.'

'Kept? Sir?'

'Yes, Inspector. Kept-kept. It is a swami who is there. From India. And that girl is saying she is wanting to be there with him for ever. He is preventing her, Inspector.'

'Preventing, sir?'

'Yes, yes. And there is worse also.'

'Sir, worse?'

'Inspector when I am sending Nirmala to California naturally I am opening bank account for her. State Bank of India, 707 Wilshire

9

Boulevard, Los Angeles.'

'Yes, sir. Naturally a father would do that. If he could.'

'But naturally also, Inspector, I am making it joint-account. Joint-account with me. So that I am always able to know-know what that girl is spending only.'

'Yes, sir, I see.'

'Inspector, she has cleared account. Every rupee, every dollar, Inspector. That man has got his hands on all. All. And, Inspector . . .'

'Yes, Mr Shahani, sir?'

'For that girl I have arranged a first-class marriage. With the son of Mr R. K. Ajmani, R. K. Ajmani and Co (Private) Ltd, import-export. That boy is very, very active and their business and mine would fit together like two cooing doves only.'

The crorepati leant forward suddenly and sharply across the huge sheet of unspotted white blotting-paper in front of him.

'Inspector,' he said, hammering out each word, 'tonight-tonight you will fly to California and there you will fetch back my daughter, whatever that damn-fool private eye is saying about happy-pappy in that ashram. You will make her see reason, Inspector, if it is taking you every day of your leave-time and twice as much more. I cannot go, Inspector. What would Shahani Enterprises do if I am not here? Mrs Shahani cannot go. Naturally she is not speaking much English. I have no one else to go. You are going to go for me, Inspector Ghote.'

CHAPTER TWO

It was very, very different from Banaras. Los Angeles airport's futuristic control tower, perched like a concrete spider on four high, shell-thin arching legs, was the first piece of California that Inspector Ghote took in, his head throbbing and dazed after hour upon hour of time-annihilating air travel.

But, he told himself, that is not something in a science-fiction magazine. It is real. It is a part of the real America, land of every sort of mechanical marvel, of space shots, of automation, of efficiency.

As he left the plane and followed his fellow passengers through the airport building, other random, equally vivid flashes impinged on him. There were tanned faces, male and female, with click-on, click-off smiles bidding him time and again 'Have a nice day'. But no nice day awaited him. That he knew with inner certainty.

And there were the enormous men everywhere, great towering muscular six-footers every one, glowing with good feeding. And girls. He had found himself standing behind two of them on a moving staircase taking him he was not quite sure where. They too were so tall, and they radiated such healthiness—easy-moving limbs, morning-fresh complexions, hair tossing freely from side to side.

How would he manage among such giants of people, people from whom high-sailing confidence shone out like the bright glow from a dance of night-time fireflies? In this ashram where Nirmala Shahani had put herself, though its head might be an Indian holy man himself perhaps an antagonist endowed with formidable mystic power, he would find her surrounded no doubt by Americans. Surrounded by Americans like the towering creatures on every side of him now, casually purposeful amid the hurly-burly of the airport, itself so different from the familiar, slow-paced, bureaucratic worm-windings of Santa Cruz Airport back at home. How would he be able to deal with such beings? To force, if necessary, answers out of them? To sift truth from the lies they might put before him? How could he fight such guardians away from the girl he had travelled so many thousands of miles to rescue?

Suddenly the universal sign for a men's room caught his eye. He broke from the steadily moving file of newly-landed passengers and plunged into it to gain a few moments' respite.

But even in this sanctuary the pressure of American life did not slacken. The whole place was relentlessly clean. It smelt, not with the familiar pungency of Bombay public lavatories but with a floweriness, an aggressive floweriness. And there was a machine for dispensing toothbrushes. *Brush regularly with Aim as part of your total oral hygiene program*, an advertisement on it commanded.

Aim, a toothpaste with an aim, a toothpaste with an undeviating purpose. And its use to be only part of a 'total oral hygiene program'. What was an oral hygiene programme even? Would he have to have one here in California? It had not been so long since he had abandoned a simple morning mouth-scrub with a sharp-smelling twig from a neem-tree in favour just of a toothbrush and a tube of *Neem* dentifrice.

He picked up his bag—Why had he not made time in Bombay to get hold of something respectably smart?—braced himself and pushed his way out back into the onward-pressing stream of passengers. There was to be, it was plain, no refuge for him anywhere in California until he had wrested Ranjee Shahani's daughter from her ashram. Not to forget as well, he cautioned himself, wresting her from the Indian swami at its head who in all probability was exercising over her power far different from the everyday cause-and-effect wrongdoing he was accustomed to deal with in Bombay.

And what about Mr Fred Hoskins?

Mr Fred Hoskins, 250 dollars a day and expenses. When Ranjee Shahani had said he

13

would cable the private eye to tell him to assist his representative from India the suggestion had been simultaneously very welcome and diabolically unpleasant. To be greeted in California by someone who knew the ways of that unknown territory, who would accept him as a properly authorized representative, there to carry out his task: that was something to be heartily grateful for. But in California to have always at his elbow, in the role of mere assistant and a discredited one at that, a man who in one day could pick up as much as two thousand rupees. Plus expenses. It was a situation so out-of-balance it would not bear thinking about.

There was the problem, too, of how he was to recognize this powerful, and discredited, figure. There had been no time to have a photograph sent from America. There had not even been time in reply to Ranjee Shahani's cable for a full personal description to be sent. What would a man who earned two thousand rupees a day look like? And, when you got down to it, all these Americans looked the same. Big.

Then, suddenly, there in front of him on a large sheet of brilliantly white card was his name, or what must be his name, boldly scrawled in thick black letters with a fat felt-pen. INSPECTOR GOTHE.

He swung his head up to look at the man holding the placard. The fellow was huge. Bigger, it seemed, even than most of the other

14

men striding by with determined, easily confident, set faces. But this fellow must be at least six foot eight. And every part of him looked proportionately large. The hands which held the placard were like two great chunks of red meat. Of beef. The face, looking challengingly over the placard's top, was of the same bloody, beefy colour and the hair crowning it, cropped close to a big square skull, was of an orangey-red hue like the fur of a jackal. But the most striking thing of all was the belly on which the lower edge of the stiff placard rested. It was tremendous. It hung forward over a well-cinched black leather belt like a great swinging sack of grain. Oh yes, much, much of those two thousand rupees per diem would be needed to fill that swaggering outgrowth.

Squaring his shoulders, Ghote went up to the giant figure.

'It is Mr Fred Hoskins?'

The big red face bent downwards. An expression of pained surprise appeared on it. A deep breath was at last drawn in.

'Inspector Goat?'

'Well, actually my name is pronounced like Go and Tay. Ghote.'

The big head nodded slowly up and down two or three times. Then the two great beef hands tore the white placard in half and in half again with two massive ripping sounds.

Fred Hoskins tossed the jagged pieces in the

15

direction of a trash basket.

What a waste only, Ghote thought briefly.

'Welcome to the greatest state of the greatest nation on earth, Inspector,' the giant suddenly boomed.

'Yes,' said Ghote. 'Yes. Thank you.'

The private eye's great red face was still looking down at him. It was plain that he was adjusting himself to a new situation.

'Okay,' the fellow said at last, with abrupt twanging certainty. 'Now, place that bag of yours in the trunk of my car and we'll proceed directly to the ashram. I had intended to introduce you around, to have you meet some of my ex-colleagues and good friends in the LAPD. But I guess not.'

LAPD? Ghote thought. Yes. Los Angeles Police Department.

He felt a little jet of pleasure at having got that right. But it hardly compensated for the certainty that he had fallen far below the private eye's expectations of any representative of the wealthy Mr Ranjee Shahani, of Bombay, India.

Oh, why had he not insisted at least on getting a new suitcase for the trip? Shahani Enterprises would have paid even.

'Yes, yes, that is a very good idea,' he said. 'The sooner I am seeing this ashram, the sooner I can be arranging for Miss Nirmala Shahani to leave.'

'You should be so lucky,' Fred Hoskins

16

banged back. 'I tell you, Inspect— Hell, I can't call you that. What's your name?'

Ghote wanted to say that his name was Ghote, and that it was spelt with the H as the second letter. But he knew at least something about Americans. They believed in informality.

'I am Ganesh,' he said. 'Ganesh.'

'Well, this is how it is, Gan,' Hoskins said. 'I'm the guy who picked up the trail of the Shahaneye kid and I'm the guy who found the ashram. So I'm in a position to inform you that I know as much about that little piece of ass as anyone. And you can take my word for it, she's not going to leave that place any time soon. She's gone off on a religion kick, and that's the way she's gonna stay.'

Ghote, his head still thickly muzzy from his long flight, felt as if a hammer was being repeatedly banged down on the top of his skull. But he had to make some sort of a reply.

'Yes, Mr Hoskins,' he began, 'I very well understand what is the position, but—'

'Listen, if we're gonna work together on this case we're gonna have to work as a team. So you're gonna have to call me Fred. In this United States we don't stand on ceremony. You're just gonna have to learn that.'

'Yes,' Ghote said.

He wished with all his might that this yammering giant could simply vanish into thin air. But he was dependent on the fellow.

17

Without him he would have the greatest difficulty getting to the ashram at all. He did not even know its address, just that it was not in Los Angeles but somewhere outside. He could make inquiries if he had to, and in the end he would find it. But if he was to act at all quickly Fred Hoskins stood, giant-like, squarely in his path.

'Fred,' he said. 'Yes, I will call you Fred.'

The big private eye led him rapidly out of the airport building to a vast car-park. Row upon row of vehicles confronted his bemused gaze, almost all huge in size, as big as any of the imported monsters belonging to Bombay film stars and a few magnates like Ranjee Shahani which swam like rare whales among the shoals of little Fiats and Ambassadors familiar to him.

Fred Hoskins directed his grain-sack of a belly down one of the dozens of alleyways between the rows of wide, grinning monsters and Ghote followed half a pace behind, leaning over to one side the better to lug his wretched-looking suitcase.

Out of the corner of his eye he registered the innumerable shiny chrome names of the cars— Chevrolet, Buick, Oldsmobile, Cadillac, Ford, Dodge, Pontiac, Peugeot, Datsun, Audi, Ferrari, BMW, Ford, Ford, Ford, Chrysler, Plymouth, Alfa-Romeo, Aston-Martin, Ford, Ford, Jaguar—a smaller vehicle this, but gleamingly expensive-looking—Toyota, Volvo, Porsche—a racing model with its name on a

18

smart red translucent panel—another Ford, another, another Chevrolet, another Cadillac, Triumph, Ford, Ford, Lotus, Saab, Ford, Ford, Ford.

So many makes, and from all over the world. So many shapes. So many colours, gold in plenty, silver, pink, scarlet, orange, the palest blue, the darkest most lustrous blue, white, black. What a fearful obstacle this very richness, number and variety seemed. So much to learn about, so much to have to deal with. What sort of a person would drive each particular make? Were there really so many people of such wealth in California? How would he ever begin to learn which car told you what about its driver? Who owned what? Who bought what? Who wanted what?

Fred Hoskins came to an abrupt halt.

'This is the bus,' he said.

It was as big as any of the monsters in the row, a huge, shiny, lurid green affair. Fred Hoskins gave its immaculate paintwork a hearty slap and then produced a bunch of keys and advanced on the driver's door. Ghote, with a cloudy notion of showing himself to be thoroughly democratic, staggered with his case round to the back and tried to lift open the hugely wide trunk.

'No! No! Wait! Wait!' Fred Hoskins yelled.

He jerked wide the door in front of him and thrust his great square jackal-fur-topped head

19

inside. From the car's interior his voice sounded just a little quieter.

'Everything automatic in this baby. Just wait right where you are.'

Ghote stood and waited, heaving in a deep breath of air.

Immediately to find lungs and throat filled with sickly, mechanical-tasting fumes so strong that his very eyes stung and watered.

He began to shake with coughing, and was only dimly aware that just in front of him the top of the big car's wide trunk was slowly rising, impressive as the portal of some massy temple.

Fred Hoskins stepped back out of the car's front door.

'Put the bag in,' he yelled. 'Let's get this show on the road.'

Coughing and spluttering, Ghote picked up his wretched case and heaved it into the trunk's vast interior.

Fred Hoskins watched him.

'You are now experiencing Los Angeles smog,' he said. 'It's the product of the vast number of vehicles on our roads. The city of Los Angeles has more cars per family than any other city in the USA. And that, I guess, goes for the world too. Coupled with the fact that the sun shines all the time in Southern California, this produces a mixture of sulphur dioxide and nitrogen oxide we call smog. D'you get it?'

'I think I have got it,' Ghote said, as yet

20

another fit of coughing shook him to the backbone.

If he was going to be like this all the time he was in California, he thought, he would never be able to summon up enough strength even to speak to Nirmala Shahani, let alone to snatch her from the grasp of her captors.

Fred Hoskins had got into the car. Ghote saw him lean forward and jab at a button somewhere.

'The door on your side is unlocked,' came that thunderous voice. 'Get the hell in here.'

Ghote hurried round, pulled open the car's immensely thick door and slid down on to the wide leather seat beside the huge private eye.

Why such a hurry, he wondered. He had agreed that it would be a good thing to get out to the ashram as soon as possible. But that had been as much out of politeness as anything. His instinct told him now that it would be a mistake in fact to go rushing in there. Rescuing Nirmala was almost certainly going to be very tricky. So he would need to be at his most alert when he arrived at the ashram. And alert he was not. His head ached and his limbs felt as if they belonged to someone else altogether.

He groped round for the handle to lower the car window beside him, thinking that once they were moving the air, smog-tainted though it was, might blow away his muzziness.

'I am going to ask you a candid question,

21

Gan,' Fred Hoskins said suddenly.

'Yes? Yes? What is it?'

'Just what the hell are you doing there?'

Ghote turned away from the padded door beside him.

'I am attempting to lower the glass only,' he said. 'I am thinking that in this heat that would be better.'

Fred Hoskins heaved a long sigh.

'Never try to open any window in this car,' he said. 'For one thing, they open automatically at the touch of a switch. And for another, you are now in an air-conditioned automobile. If any passenger opens a window, the cool air from the air-conditioner right in front of you escapes outside. Now, watch this.'

A thick beef-red finger jabbed at one of the rows of buttons on the long, gleaming dashboard and at once through a small vent at about midriff level there came a blast of ice-cold air.

'Very good, very good,' Ghote gasped.

He wondered whether on top of all his other troubles he was now going to catch a chill.

Fred Hoskins eased the battleship car out of its place and took it along the interminable row of other huge vehicles towards the park exit.

'Please,' Ghote asked, 'how far is it to the ashram?'

They might be there in half an hour or less. Would he possibly be fit enough to tackle the

22

swami who ruled the place? And whatever tribe of enormous Americans he had gathered round him?

The big private eye gave him no answer. His eyes were fixed on another car approaching the exit from a different direction and a foot or two in advance.

'See those plates?' he muttered. 'Ohio plates. I'm not gonna let a hick like that get outa here in front of me.'

The lurid green battleship lurched suddenly forward. Through the firmly closed window beside him Ghote heard a squeal of brakes. He twisted round to see what had happened. The hick from Ohio had brought his vehicle to a stop and was shaking his fist. Fred Hoskins gunned his motor and they shot out of the park.

'When you get to drive in California, Gan boy, you gotta be aggressive.'

'Yes.'

Ghote decided not to ask again how far the ashram was for at least a few minutes.

He watched the streets outside. They were very different from those at home, but he found it hard to say exactly why. There were big buildings in the Fort area of Bombay much as there were here and indeed many of those he could see did not look much newer or smarter than some there. But there was a difference, a strong difference.

And then it came to him. It was the people,

23

the way they were moving. No one was just standing, much less sitting or lying asleep on the pavement as they would be in Bombay. Everyone he saw seemed to be going somewhere in a determined manner. Yes, that was it. This was a place full of purpose. A place where time was money.

And the cars all around them. Fred Hoskins's butting driving style was only a shade more forceful than every other driver's. Bombay wallahs in charge of a car could do things that were hair-raising enough, especially say a Sikh behind the wheel of a taxi. But here people were not just taking occasional mad risks. They were pushing and pressing ceaselessly with steady, confident determination one against the other.

If he had not had Fred Hoskins to take him to his destination, how would he have managed in conditions like this? Could he have produced that aggressiveness the private eye had said was so necessary here?

Despite the beating in his head and that faraway feeling in his legs, he made up his mind that if he ever did have to drive in California, dammit, he would push with the best of them.

'Mr Hosk—Fred,' he said, 'how far is it, please, to the ashram?'

'Not far. It's just about on the County limit. About sixty or seventy, I guess.'

All that way. Nirmala Shahani must be hidden in the deepest countryside somewhere.

24

'That is sixty-seventy kilometres?' he asked.

'Miles. Seventy good honest American miles, boy.'

Seventy miles.

'But, please, how long will it take to get there then?'

Ghote looked at his watch. But the time it showed seemed to bear no relation to anything. Had he altered the hands when the plane was coming into Los Angeles? He could not remember.

He tried to look up through the car's lightly greyed windows to see the sun. But with the smog haze thick above he could not make out at all where in the sky it might be.

'In this bus,' Fred Hoskins said, giving the wide moulded wheel in front of him an emphatic smack with a great red beefy hand, 'no time at all. But I'm gonna give you a tour of the real LA before we hit the freeway.'

'Oh? Yes. Thank you.'

Ghote sat wondering what on earth was happening. A few minutes ago Fred Hoskins had been furiously impatient to be on their way. Now he was talking about making a sight-seeing detour.

But he was in the fellow's hands altogether. Nirmala Shahani was held in the ashram, seventy miles away in what direction he did not know. If he was to get to her without interminable delays he had to rely on this

25

clamorous giant of a man, however many times the fellow seemed to change his mind.

Sending the big green car weaving forcefully through the lanes of traffic, Fred Hoskins began to talk.

'Gan, boy, you're gonna thank me for what I'm about to do for you. You're gonna see for yourself the classiest community in all Southern California. I'm gonna take you through Beverly Hills, home of many world-famous stars of the motion-picture industry. Beverly Hills is a city. And you've got to get this right: it's legally separate from LA although it's still a suburb. And in Beverly Hills you'll find some of the most luxurious homes in the world.'

A driver almost as aggressive as the big private eye attempted at this moment to cut in ahead of them and the thump-thumping flow of words temporarily came to a halt. Ghote decided that perhaps he ought to offer something of his own.

'In Bombay also,' he said, 'our film stars are having most posh homes.'

'As I was saying, Gan, the most luxurious homes in the world, owned by the world's classiest people. We're now driving along La Cienga Boulevard—when incompetent drivers let us—but soon we'll make a left on to Sunset Boulevard. Sunset Boulevard is a name you'll certainly recall. It was the title of a famous movie featuring Gloria Swanson. In case you

26

didn't catch it in a movie theatre, you'll have seen it on your local television station many, many times.'

The voice hammered on and on, each syllable setting up a new thud in Ghote's head. He thought for a brief moment of trying to explain that American films were not shown on Bombay Doordarshan and that in any case he himself had no set. But by now he had realized that even if he succeeded in getting in a few words about Indian television this giant at the wheel of his giant car would not hear him.

He turned instead to thinking about his coming encounter with the swami holding Nirmala Shahani and the bodyguard of enormous Americans that he would in all likelihood have round him. What could he himself do, despite the swimmy fatigue that had invaded his every limb, to prepare for the encounter?

Precious little, he recognized soon enough. All he knew about the swami was the fact, reported to Ranjee Shahani by Fred Hoskins, that he was known in California simply as the Swami With No Name. Any name, he had explained in an interview the private eye had found in the files of the *Los Angeles Times*, was a link with the world and he had long been free of all earthly ties.

It was a considerable claim. And it might, just possibly, be true. There were such men in

27

India, the yogis, those who had taken the path to things unimaginably high. But in California? An Indian setting himself up as a swami in California, was it not more likely that he was nothing other than a confidence trickster? That name that was no name was just the sort of thing to impress people who had no knowledge of Indian philosophy, and it would serve nicely too to protect the fellow from awkward inquiries.

But, trickster or genuine yogi, one thing was clear; the Swami With No Name was not going to be easy to tackle.

'We are now entering the city limits of Beverly Hills.' Fred Hoskins's slam-bang voice broke in on his thoughts.

He sat up and did his best to look as if he was delightedly taking in everything he saw. He must do what he could to keep the giant beside him on his side. They were going to be a team. The fellow had said so at the airport. He felt the thought descend like a mass of half-chewed chapatti to the pit of his stomach.

Oh, if only he could accomplish his mission in two or three hours of sweeping activity. End up, before this day was done, with a rescued Nirmala Shahani ready to fly at his side back to Bombay, to her father, to the arranged marriage awaiting her with the heir to R. K. Ajmani, import-export.

Dutifully he regarded the stately houses set back far from the road, itself bordered, not by

28

pavements for people to walk along, but by wide, beautifully trimmed, implacably green lawns laid to separate the homes from the cars.

A niggle of doubt struck him.

Surely Fred Hoskins had declared that the sun shone without interruption in Southern California. How could it be then that these lawns were so green? In Bombay, where outside the monsoon months the sun also shone unrelentingly, grass on such open spaces as the maidans was always a uniform parched brown.

'Please,' he said, 'how is it that these lawns I am seeing are altogether of such a fine green hue?'

'Sprinklers, Gan. Every day for about an hour these lawns will get a continuous sprinkling from pipes in the ground. The water comes from mighty reservoirs built in the hills which surround Los Angeles. They are some of the major engineering feats of the world.'

'Yes,' Ghote said, putting his head mentally between his arms to protect himself from the rain of hammer blows.

He made up his mind not to ask another single question, however much silence might cost him in his relations with the towering private eye.

He sat pretending to be dumbstruck with amazement at the size and magnificence of the houses to either side, at spreading red-tiled roofs that reminded him of a little Catholic enclave he

29

knew in Bombay only multiplied ten or twenty fold, at great white-pillared façades, at wide green gardens under gracefully bending palm trees.

Yet somehow even these palms were different. They ought to have been reassuringly familiar. But they lacked altogether the battered dustiness of the palm trees of Bombay.

He felt very far from home. A venturer making his way through territory that could all too easily hide every kind of unknown trap. And his only companion this giant beside him. Who seemed as much enemy as friend.

CHAPTER THREE

Uneasily Ghote looked at the jutting-bellied private eye grasping the wheel of his monster car. The fellow ought to be simply a help to him. Ranjee Shahani must be paying him two thousand rupees a day still to be exactly that. Yet his attitude so far had not really been at all helpful. He seemed to be an obstacle in the way, making things difficult, refusing to answer questions. He was yet one more hard hill to climb in a whole series of mountain ridges he felt lying between him and Ranjee Shahani's daughter.

Why was the fellow behaving like this?

But the thumping muzziness in his head would not let him work his way to any clear answer. Perhaps, after all, it was no more than the fact that the fellow was so American, so Californian. There was this huge car of his. There was his enormous well-fed frame. There was his aggressiveness and that seemingly unshakable confidence in the kind of life he was living. Yes, perhaps it was just that the fellow summed up in himself this whole rich, different land.

And now another of those great, tumbling speeches was beginning.

'We're now climbing.' Not that this was not perfectly evident, even though the huge car apparently needed no shifting of its gears to tackle the steep rise in the road ahead. 'These are the Santa Monica Mountains. You'll notice that even in this inhospitable terrain the citizens of Los Angeles have established their homes, striving to rise above the smog that stifles the city at sea-level. Now, look to your left. There on the hillside you'll see a magnificent residence built on steel stilts to conform to the slope. Note that even at this distance from other homes the house is fully equipped with electrical power and is connected by pipeline to the city water supply.'

Ghote looked to the left. Yes, the stark white house on the hillside was raised up on stilts.

'Who is the owner of such a fine

31

establishment?' he asked, at once breaking his just imposed rule about asking questions.

'In a few moments,' Fred Hoskins replied, massively ignoring his question, 'I will tell you to turn your eyes to the right. By that time we'll have ascended the full height of the mountains and on the far side you'll have a view of the famed San Fernando Valley. I will not at this time sing you the song of that name.'

A spasm of anger shook Ghote from the base of his spine to the top of his ever more heavily thudding head.

'Mr Hoskins,' he said, 'kindly tell me. In the course of your inquiries on behalf of Mr Ranjee Shahani did you interview the Swami With No Name himself?'

But again the hulking private eye ignored his question, leaving instead a massive silence in the big car.

Ghote, his anger yet more fuelled, would not have let him get away with it. Except that at that moment there came into view around a bend in the twisting road ahead an extraordinary sight.

It was a man. A man coming towards them close to the edge of the road, a road here as elsewhere without any sidewalk. He was running, thumping along at a steady even pace. And he was dressed in the smallest imaginable pair of bright red, shiny satin shorts topped by a white T-shirt with a printed message on it in red letters so big that Ghote had taken them in at a

32

single glance. FIGHT THE FAT. On the runner's feet were bright red-and-white shoes and round his head were what could only be headphones, a pair of huge headphones like two black dishes clamped over either ear.

Fred Hoskins, who since Ghote's question had been concentrating ferociously on the wheel in front of him, appeared not even to have noticed the sight.

'That—that person,' Ghote said, as the big car moved past the runner, 'what—what is he?'

'What person, Gan? Can't you see I'm concentrating on the road?'

'There was a man in the road. Someone running. You would see him still in your mirror.'

Fred Hoskins jabbed a glance at the mirror.

'Jogger,' he said.

'Please, what is a jogger?'

'Jeez, Gan boy, where'd you come from? A jogger's a guy who needs to cut down on the flab. So he gets out there and buys himself a pair of running shoes and some shorts from one of the stores especially for joggers and then he hits the road and pounds that extra flesh into the ground.'

'I see,' Ghote said.

He thought of asking whether it would not be better not to eat so much in the first place. But he felt that in his present jet-confused state he could not trust himself to put the question in a properly polite manner.

'And was that a pair of headphones he was wearing also?' he asked. 'Please what is the purpose of those?'

'Music on the move, Gan. From radio stations strategically placed so no American needs to be without music at any time of the night or day. Rock music, country music, sweet music, pop music—all or any of these are there for him at the touch of a button.'

'In India also—'

But they had arrived at the crest of the hill.

'Look, Gan, look. For Christ's sake, look, won't you?'

'Yes, yes. I am looking.'

Fred Hoskins brought his enormous car to a halt just off the road, its wide front pointing at the valley spread below.

'Gan boy,' he demanded, 'is that or is that not a truly memorable view?'

It was certainly a huge extent of country that lay spread out before them. And behind as well it was possible to see for as far as twenty miles or more, though there the scene was for the most part obscured by the smog. In front, however, everything was clear. Far below, tiny, thin roads crossed and re-crossed in a huge grid pattern, with little bright beads of colour moving along them everywhere, sometimes in long necklaces, elsewhere as minuscule individual beetles. Above, against a purely blue sky planes by the

34

dozen buzzed to and fro like so many purposeful bees.

Ghote turned to the private eye.

'Yes, Fred,' he said. 'A truly marvellous sight. But, tell me please, were you at any time having an interview with the Swami With No Name?'

The private eye yanked furiously at his car's starter-key, slammed at a lever and shot the machine suddenly backwards on to the road again. Then, as poundingly, he hurled the car into forward and plunged off down the hill in front of them.

'Mr Hoskins,' Ghote said adamantly, 'did you see the swami?'

'There just wasn't any need,' Fred Hoskins answered at last, peering through the windscreen in front of him as if he was by no means the domineeringly confident driver he had shown himself to be up to now but some spinster lady setting out for her very first drive. 'I saw the Shahaneye kid, didn't I? I put her father's heartfelt plea to her. I put it to her straight. And she just doesn't want to go back home. Period. Finito. That's it.'

'Yes,' Ghote said.

Mechanically he looked round him as they twisted down the sharp hill at a speed now he felt must surely be reckless. There were houses again though these were set yet further back from the road because of the steepness of the

35

slope. And then there were every now and again extraordinary squares of high walls, black, plastic and mysterious, set with what looked like portholes. What could they be? A sudden jump of the imagination gave it to him. They were tennis-courts. Yes, tennis courts surrounded by high mesh walls. And practically every other house had one.

What a country, what a tremendous, rich-to-bursting country. It was not just a land where time was money: it was a land where money was play.

And it was supporting—in some way, he felt, as the topmost jewel on a pyramid of richly gleaming gems—the Swami With No Name. The man that Fred Hoskins, despite his two thousand rupees a day plus expenses, had not succeeded in obtaining an interview with.

Well, at least the fellow had ceased that incessant yammering.

Ghote shut his eyes and hoped that in the quiet the steady thudding in his head would gradually calm down. The big car had soon entered the freeway—for a few moments Ghote had dazedly regarded the great sweep of the eight-lane road in front of him, but soon he had fallen back into his doze—and for minute after minute now they zoomed along with only the muted booming of the car's powerful engine breaking the silence.

Resolutely Ghote refused to let himself think

any more about the ashram that lay at the end of this journey. It was no use, he decided, trying to guess what the situation there would be like. Worrying about it would only worsen his headache.

But, whatever efforts he made to drop completely into a healing sleep, he was unable to shake off the malaise that afflicted him. There was a slight feeling of sickness in the pit of his stomach. His limbs still seemed to be elsewhere. His temples thudded.

So from time to time he cautiously opened his eyes.

The sights he saw did nothing to bring to an end the pervasive feeling of unreality. Even before they had got on to the endless stretch of the freeway he had had his first shock.

There had been an alteration in the big car's speed. He had glanced out. And there ahead, just off the road to his right, he had seen, soaring up into the sky, an enormous double arch of pure gold.

The ashram, he had thought at once. We are there. I must have been sound asleep. The ashram. Oh, my God.

'Please, please. We have arrived?'

'What the heck?'

'But that—' He had jerked his head in the direction of the pure shining arch—'It is the ashram?'

'Gan boy that is a McDonald's. That's the

sign of a McDonald's. The fast food chain. Don't you have those in India?'

The tone of disparagement was so crushing that all he had been able to do was to murmur some apology, something about being asleep and dreaming, and shut his eyes tight once again. He had taken that one other glimpse out when they had got on to the freeway—eight lanes, eight lanes of roadway and each of them humming with traffic—and then had done his best to blot out everything.

But in vain.

His inner uneasiness woke him to find himself looking straight at a huge thundering truck made in the form of a great bread-roll with an enormous sausage stuck between its two halves, oozing with bright yellow plastic mustard some five or six inches thick. A hot dog. At least he knew enough about the American way of life to recognize that. But such a gigantic advertisement, and whamming along the freeway at—it must be—seventy miles an hour.

Fred Hoskins's car purred past the extraordinary sight, and Ghote shut his eyes again.

To open them once more to see the sweeping road in front of them splitting into two quite different sections as they climbed a mountain range and on the far section, some fifty feet above them on the hillside, a whole procession of cars was descending at speed, each one of

38

them topped by a bright-coloured shape fastened to its roof which, as he closed his eyes firmly once again, he realized were surfboards.

All those people, going all that way, at such a speed, to take those hugely expensive-looking pieces of shaped wood to play with at the ocean side. The land where money was play. And where, surely, one whole group of these huge, confident people were playing at being a swami's disciples.

But, no, no, no. He must not think about that.

Peace and calm. That was what would get rid of this pounding in his head, this detachedness in his limbs.

In another glimpse he saw a huge double-tanker, all gleaming steel, toiling just ahead of them up the mountain. And had it really been that, as they had zoomed smoothly past, Fred Hoskins had uttered the single word 'Milk'? Was each one of these enormous tanks full up to the brim with milk? Milk from heaven knows how many cows? Could there be that much milk? And ahead of the milk-tanker had there really been a huge trailer with no fewer than ten new cars on it? Cars being carried?

No, it was not a dream. It was not. Try as he might, he had not been able to get properly to sleep.

Then there was a house being swept along on a trailer, down on the far side of the mountain now. A house? Certainly half a house, a wooden house complete with curtains at its windows, flapping like sails in a stiff breeze, and wallpaper to be glimpsed in the interior.

Then, not on the unending road itself but down beside a farmstead some fifty yards from it, casually left as if it was a battered old lorry, there was a plane. A plane in a farmyard. It must be a dream. It was not.

He made himself then keep his eyes open for a little, taking care to hold himself so that Fred Hoskins could not see that he was awake. Another word-battering from the jackal-fur-crowned private eye and his throbbing head would split.

From the twisted angle he was looking down on to the road he began to notice what lay on the verge just beside it. For yard on yard it was littered by rubbish. There were bright drinks cans of every colour, some crumpled, others intact and rolling a little to and fro in the wind of the passing speeding vehicles. There were bottles, glinting in the sun intact or broken into a thousand glittering fragments, there were, sparkling white and indestructible, dozens and dozens and dozens of little beakers made out of some substance so light that they drifted backwards and forwards in the slightest puff of air. Throwaway cups. But unlike the clay cups of India they seemed obstinately to resist going back into their native element. And there were

40

too, cardboard boxes, hundreds of them, brightly coloured, which he surmised must have contained things to eat, those hot dogs or whatever it was you got at that Mc—Yes, McDonald's.

How stupid he had been over that. What an advantage he had given to Two Thousand Rupees A Day, plus expenses. To the Californian.

He shut his eyes once more to blot out the thought.

But he could not keep them closed for long.

Eat All You Want, To the right, a little way off the eight striding lanes of the huge road where a turn-off led to a gas-station, these four words painted enormously on a huge signboard vibrated in his sight. Eat all you want. An invitation to anyone. What riches, what extravagance.

He shuddered.

But within minutes—Or had he this time succeeded in dozing a little before opening his eyes?—another sign blared into his consciousness. A warning notice. *Speed Checked By Aircraft.*

To have enough resources to keep aircraft flying above this immense sweeping road to measure the speed of the hundreds of tearaway vehicles thundering along it. What a country he had come to. How things worked here. How the cars and the trucks zooming along beside them,

41

breaking the speed-limit no doubt, ran sweetly with, it seemed, never a rattle, never any clouds of overheated steam, never a grinding thump and a long halt by the roadside. And this green monster in which he was sitting. It too had worked perfectly in every respect. The huge trunk had opened smoothly at the touch of a button for him to put his case in. His door had been unlocked at the touch of another button with not a sign of jamming. The air-conditioning had blasted coldly out the moment Fred Hoskins had switched it on, and it had continued to pour a chill breeze on to him ever since. Everything worked. How oppressive that was.

Suddenly, however, the lulling tempo of the big speeding car was checked. Ghote sat up, shaking his head and looking all around him. He had slept. He must have done. Because they had left the freeway and were going at a much reduced speed along a quite narrow blacktop road.

'Just about one mile to go, Gan boy,' Fred Hoskins said, his hammer voice bringing home to Ghote that sleep had done nothing to cure his thudding head. 'I estimate our journey time at one hour and thirty-eight minutes. Some driving.'

'Oh, yes. Good. Very good. Fred.'

Ghote felt a sudden hollow in the pit of his stomach. In just a few minutes' time he might find himself confronting the Swami With No Name. And what would he say to him? How would he be able, in these strange, upsetting surroundings, to decide whether or not he was talking to a true swami, a yogi, a person who had acquired powers that could be at their highest nothing short of miraculous? Or, if the man was not a yogi, would he even be able, feeling wretched as he did, to catch him out in his fraud? Because no doubt about it, if he was a fraudster he would be a devilishly cunning one.

And which of those two alternatives would it be preferable to find?

He wriggled on the broad leather seat of the monster car.

Perhaps, after all, he would be lucky and be prevented from meeting this adversary straight away. Perhaps it would be only Nirmala Shahani that he would have to tackle. A mere girl, whose obstinacy surely would not be too difficult to overcome, even if it took some days of persuasive talk.

And the ashram, what would that be like? Would it be a familiar Indian place, even though that sort of establishment was one he ordinarily fought shy of? A cluster of huts, with the swami's a little bigger than the rest? A tree to give some shade? A kitchen with sharp-smelling cowdung smoke rising up from it? Disciples in orange robes or orange saris sitting cross-legged on the ground listening to the long, sweet

43

discourse of their guru, with a goat or two and some chickens wandering in among them?

Or would it be an American ashram? Something hard indeed to picture, but full of the great, tall creatures he had seen, confident, swift-moving, dealing with religion in just the same way as they dealt with the business of leaving the airport or the play of jogging or of tennis?

Would such people stand like guards keeping Nirmala away from him? Would they call in the cops when he tried to approach her? Accuse him of attempted abduction?

Or would they leave the Swami to deal with him? Either by powers there could be no resisting, or by some double-dealing that, here alone, he would find hard to counter?

Fred Hoskins had brought the car almost to a halt. There was a gateway set a little back in the fence bordering the road and beside it a large white signboard with painted on it in rose-pink letters the single word 'Ashram'.

Ghote swallowed, dry-mouthed. His head gave a series of pain-darting thumps.

They turned in through the open gate and went slowly along a dirt track. Soon, just before they entered the shade of the tall, dark green redwood trees that rose all the way up the ridge in front of them, they saw a low, circular, log-walled hut. Fred Hoskins pulled up in front of it.

'We have now arrived at the ashram Visitors Centre,' he announced, his voice booming even more loudly in the surrounding quiet. 'This was the site of my interview with the Shahaneye girl. An interview, as you will recall, during which she informed me clearly that she never wished to return to Bombay, India. I came to the conclusion at that time, thanks to my training as a member of the LAPD, that the witness was speaking the entire truth.'

'Yes,' Ghote said. 'But of course, I must see her also. And the Swami, too.'

'It's what you're here for, Gan. I suggest you now proceed into the Visitors Centre and start your inquiries. I'll stay here as your back-up. Are you packing anything?'

Ghote, half way out of the huge car, turned back.

'My suitcase, is it?' he asked, more than a little dazed. 'You think I should take it with me?'

'A piece, Gan. A piece. I asked if you're packing a piece.'

A feeling of total bewilderment descended on Ghote.

'Please,' he asked, 'a piece of what?'

The look of pained dismay that he had seen on the towering private eye's great beef-red face when they had first met reappeared and was even more explicit.

'A piece, Gan. Are you carrying a gun?'

45

'No,' Ghote said. 'No, I am not. But why should I? I cannot take the girl away from here at gunpoint only. I am a policeman, not one of your gangster fellows.'

'A police officer,' Fred Hoskins said, his booming voice incredulous. 'A cop without a piece.' He heaved a tremendous sigh. 'Well, it's your case, I guess, Inspector Goat.'

Ghote turned away and stepped clear of the car.

Yes, it was his case. Whatever way it had been thrust on to him, it was his case. If Nirmala Shahani was being detained at this place wrongfully, whether through some mystical power or by means of trickery, then he was going to find out exactly what had been done to her and take her away with him back to her rightful home. Ranjee Shahani had been certain his daughter was an unwilling victim and, even though influence had been used to secure altogether special attention, it was still right that there should be an investigation.

And investigation was his job. He would do it. Here in this extraordinary, burstingly wealthy land, just as he would do it in the familiar heights and depths of dusty Bombay.

He marched across towards the Visitors Centre.

When he got to within a few yards of the building he saw that its double doors were standing wide open. Ridiculously, the fact at

46

once disturbed him. He saw himself as confronted by some jungle monkey-trap. The moment curiosity had lured him inside, he felt, those doors would come flapping closed behind him and he would be, not shipped off to some money-splurging research establishment across the other side of the world, but certainly somehow prevented from carrying out the task he had come here to do.

He gave his steadily thudding head a little angry shake. What absurdities entered in when the mind was disoriented.

A few brisk steps took him inside the little building. To his surprise there was no one there. He looked round. The walls were largely hidden by clothes racks on which hung loose orangey-coloured garments, each marked with a prominent price-tag. A pair of large glass-fronted cupboards also contained various labelled items for sale. *Electronic Meditation Timer*, he read. *Shanti Board Game (Non-Competitive)*. *Yoga Pants (Guaranteed Made in India)*—the price asked for those simple garments made him raise his eyebrows— *Meditation Earplugs (Natural Wax)*, *Folding Meditation Bench (Cushion Extra)*.

The middle of the hut was occupied by an eight-sided table on which various brightly-coloured pamphlets had been spread in neat piles. Up against one of the piles, he saw, there was a piece of card with something written on it in scrawled letters. He bent forward more closely and read.

Swami is giving a discourse in the Meditation Hall this afternoon. All Visitors Welcome. Follow the path up the hill.

He felt a jet of pleasure. The Swami Without A Name giving a discourse. It would provide a first-class opportunity to take a good, long look at the fellow while he himself was unobserved. Just what he wanted.

And—suddenly things were going his way—there behind one of the racks of floppy orange garments was a little back-door to the hut. If he could slip out through that he might be able to leave Fred Hoskins sitting in his monster car as—what was it he had said?—a back-up. With his piece, yes, his piece at the ready. To be free of that looming, noisy presence while making some quiet observations, what could be better?

The little door proved to be unlocked. Ghote stepped carefully out and began to make his way through the tall redwood trees up the hill, carefully keeping the bulk of the Visitors Centre between himself and Fred Hoskins's car.

Soon after he had safely rejoined the dirt track he began to see through the trees the shapes of bright-coloured tents and the occasional wooden hut. He guessed that these were where the disciples of the ashram slept. Perhaps in one of them Nirmala Shahani would be found.

After a while the broad path, criss-crossed

48

with tyre-tracks, divided, one branch continuing
straight up the hill and the other, marked with a
neat signpost saying 'Ashram', leading off to the
right. A few yards distant from the fork a
curious little structure caught his eye. It looked
like a square metal cupboard standing all alone,
half-hidden by the thick trunk of a soaring
redwood. It was painted a bright blue and had
some white lettering on it.

He wondered if it might be some sort of
information kiosk, somewhere with pamphlets
about the ashram and perhaps some bio-data on
the Swami With No Name. He ought to have
taken whatever was available at the Visitors
Centre, but the prospect of slipping away and
seeing the Swami quietly for himself had made
him forget. This might be his chance.

He went quickly through the trees towards
the upright little metal box, and when he got
near was able to see that the lettering on it spelt
out *Johnny All Alone*. What could that mean?

Cautiously he pulled open the door at the
front.

A lavatory, western-style, confronted him,
smelling abundantly of some artificial
floweriness, very like that he had encountered in
the men's room at the airport, an American
smell. The disappointment and surprise affected
him with altogether disproportionate force.
Abruptly he was aware how very far away he
was from India. Poor, distant India where for

the most part the open ground, though perhaps it should not be so, served the purpose of this bright blue box, so efficient, so functional and so private.

At a much slower pace he made his way along the path leading to the ashram's Meditation Hall and the Swami With No Name.

He did not have far to go before he saw through the trees a circle of large log-built huts with, rising above them two odd and different buildings. One, on the further side of the circle, was a big, pure white dome looking to his eyes a cross between a futuristic, solidly material structure reminiscent in a way of the spider-like control tower at Los Angeles airport and something airily light and flyaway like the intangible spiritual claims of an ashram.

But the second, nearer structure was perhaps even odder. At its base, he saw as he advanced, it was a log-cabin much like the Visitors Centre though somewhat larger, square in shape and apparently without windows. Above this base, however, there rose, twice as high, into the unbroken deep blue of the sky a tall spiral apparently made out of translucent orange plastic. What could such a place be?

He would have to find out later. The opportunity of observing the Swami awaited him urgently now.

He went forward until he had reached the edge of the wide clearing in which the circle of

50

buildings stood. There could be little doubt that the big white dome was the Meditation Hall and, squaring his shoulders, he set off towards it passing through the gap between the extraordinary orange-roofed building and a large plain one which, to judge by the faint odour of food coming from it, would be the ashram's communal dining hall.

Against its wall, just as he emerged into the centre circle, a bicycle was propped in a state of half-repair, the tyre of its front wheel off and the soft rubber inner-tube loosely dangling. It was a machine of much the same old standard pattern as the thousands he saw every day on the streets of Bombay, markedly different from the one or two low-slung, heavily-geared affairs he had noticed at the start of his trip out to the ashram. The sight of this old machine reversed in an instant the depression he had been plunged into by his encounter with the Johnny-All-Alone box. Here at last was something that did not work, and someone who, clearly, had lost heart half-way through trying to put it to rights.

Perhaps, here under the Californian sun, he was after all in a sort of India.

So he marched, careless now of his still thud-thudding head, straight across the centre circle over to the pure whiteness of the domed Meditation Hall. Its double doors, like those of the Visitors Centre, stood invitingly open. But this time he did not hesitate, mounted the two

51

or three wooden steps confidently and entered.

He found himself in a lobby whose floor was covered with a huge variety of footwear, sandals, shoes, boots, runner's shoes like the pair he had seen on the jogger and great clumsy rubber boots, all discarded in obedience to a stark notice on the wall saying *Abandon Shoes and Logic All Ye Who Enter Here*.

But he was not going to abandon logic. Certainly not. He was going to enter and observe and quietly deduce. He was going to be what Dr Hans Gross called in his mildew-stained masterwork *Criminal Investigation*, which he had not succeeded in snatching before his departure from his cabin at CID Headquarters, 'a careful weigher of facts'.

His shoes, however, he would abandon. He did not want in any way to be conspicuous inside the hall.

He slipped them off—they were his better pair, worn in honour and fear of setting foot in America—put them where he could slide into them again quickly and easily and then turned to the inner pair of double doors leading into the hall itself.

Very quietly he pushed back one leaf and stepped inside.

The sight that met his eyes was as reassuring as the half-repaired bicycle had been. Under its white dome the building looked not all that unlike a temple in India. It was a good deal more filled with light, but the whole floor area was cluttered with worshippers, most of them sitting cross-legged. Many wore clothes, either orange in colour or white, that might have been seen in any temple, though here and there some unashamed westerners were dressed in T-shirts. On the far wall in huge Devanagri script was the mystic word '*Aum*' together with paintings that plainly represented swamis of a past era, men who had never left their native India, copiously white-bearded sages whose eyes glowed with tender thoughts. And they were garlanded, too.

The air was heavy as well with the scent of *agarbati*, the drifting smoke from the little burning sticks visible here and there. And there was sitar music, rolling and tinkling out. Evidently the Swami had yet to begin his discourse.

All the better.

He dropped into a sitting position on the floor by the doors.

The sitar-player, when he had located him at the left-hand front corner of the raised platform at the far side of the hall, gave him a new jab of uneasiness. Although dressed in the ochre garb of a holy man and although his playing gave .every evidence of familiarity with his instrument, he was unmistakably a Westerner. His shaven head, all but a tuft at the back, was white-skinned and pale and his deep-set eyes were a piercingly bright blue.

53

The steady thudding of his headache obtruded itself again and he was once more aware of the weariness deep in every limb.

And then suddenly his eyes were caught by the man he had come to observe, and had a little dreaded seeing. The Swami With No Name. At the opposite side of the platform to the white sitar-player he had quietly risen to his feet. But smooth and apparently unobtrusive though the movement had been, somehow it had at once attracted the gaze of every person down on the floor of the big domed building.

Perhaps, Ghote told himself sharply, this was simply because there had come the moment in a regular order of events when the Swami's discourse always began. So his hungry audience would have been expecting him to get to his feet. Perhaps no more than that was needed to explain the mass magnetic movement down on the floor. Or perhaps not.

The Swami stood looking silently down on the sea of upturned faces. At the other side of the platform the sitar music faded away into nothingness.

Ghote had to acknowledge that the man, true yogi or clever confidence trickster, was an impressive figure. Heavy curling locks of black hair fell tumbling on either side of a clean-shaven, full face that gave out a sweetness and benevolence which radiated to the very furthest points of the big domed building. He was tall,

54

too. Tall and upstanding with broad, easily-held shoulders. He wore clothes of the same orange as most of the people sitting at his feet. But it was plain to see even at a distance, that where they were dressed in cotton he was clad from head to foot in silk. A loose top-garment, loose trousers and a wide shawl across his broad shoulders in a shade of orange that was almost red.

Yes, no getting away from it, an impressive figure.

And now, after a long, long pause, he was raising his curl-framed head to speak.

What would he say? Would he produce a stream of honeyed comfort such as the swamis on Chowpatty Beach back in Bombay poured out to their attentive hearers on the dry sand in front of them? Or would he produce something different. Something somehow American?

The words the Swami uttered as he began were neither of those. And they astonished Ghote.

'There is someone here in pain,' he said. 'Someone who has come and is not happy. His head is paining him. He needs help. You there, at the back by the doors, come here to me.'

CHAPTER FOUR

Could the Swami's summons be for someone else? How at such a distance had he come to know that there had entered the Meditation Hall somebody whose head was indeed thudding with pain? Would he come to know in just the same way when they were face to face that this was someone who had journeyed so many thousands of miles for the sole purpose of entering into contest with him? And if he did, surely he would be able to win the encounter there and then.

Faces all over the hall were turned in Ghote's direction. The people sitting on the floor nearest him—some, he noticed absurdly, had small bouncy cushions under them—were beginning to encourage him with little gestures and warm-beaming smiles to get to his feet and go forward.

A spasm of rage jerked through him.

He shot up and strode furiously towards the corner of the platform where the Swami With No Name stood smilingly awaiting him.

Then, at last, they were face to face.

The Swami did not speak a word. Instead he put out his right hand and laid it on Ghote's shoulder, quite close to the neck. Ghote at once felt a sensation of peculiar warmth there. It was something quite different, much more active than the warmth that might have been expected this warm, sunny Californian afternoon from a hand, even a rather plump hand. It was as if, he felt, there was an actual source of heat within that dense, soft flesh.

And immediately all the weariness and grittiness accumulated over hours of being swept through the skies at hundreds of miles an hour began seeping out of him through, it seemed, some sump-hole in the back of his neck. All the hours of having time rush backwards past him sapping at his energies were within moments forgotten. The hours he had spent breathing sterile air until the spring of life in him seemed choked were in an instant obliterated. He felt as well as he had ever done in his life.

Damn the man. Damn him, damn him, he thought savagely, his eyes looking straight at the gently swelling orange silk that hid a well-rounded stomach.

Damn him. Why should he be endowed with a power like this? A power which at a stroke had put him himself completely at a disadvantage? How would it be possible now to interrogate the fellow as if he were some ordinary suspect hauled into CID Headquarters at Crawford Market? How could he ask him sharp questions about the circumstances in which Nirmala Shahani had come to his ashram? How could he ask whether and how often he had seen the girl alone? How could he demand that the fellow account for the large sum removed from the State Bank of India, 707 Wilshire Boulevard?

How could he even insist that he himself had a private interview with Ranjee Shahani's daughter before anybody here had an opportunity to prepare her?

'Sit now,' the Swami said suddenly, in a low cooing voice. 'Sit here just by me. You will be my favourite this afternoon.'

Slowly Ghote lowered himself to a sitting position just beside the low platform within a few inches of where the Swami's bare feet were softly planted. Furiously he registered that he was actually feeling a sense of privilege at being the nearest person in the whole hall to him.

He clenched his fists and made a deliberate, fierce effort to remove himself from the fellow's influence.

I am Ganesh Ghote, he forced his mind to hammer out. I am an Inspector of the Bombay CID. I have been sent to this place on the orders of my superior officer to fulfil a request by a citizen of Bombay with the right to make it—or at least with the influence necessary—to investigate whether his daughter, Nirmala Shahani by name, is or is not being detained here against her will. Unless I find altogether satisfactory evidence that she is here of her own free will I intend to take her back with me to Bombay, there to hand over to her concerned father so that she can make the marriage he has arranged for her to the mutual advantage of the families on both sides. And afterwards she will live an ordinary, simple life, happy at some times, less happy at others. But the life that she was born to.

I am Inspector Ghote, and I will see that this happens.

So was Nirmala Shahani here now somewhere? Almost certainly she must be.

Careful not to make any conspicuous movement, he began a cautious survey of the attentive upward-turned faces in front of him. From the platform above the Swami launched into his promised discourse like a wide-bowed ship gently descending into waiting waters.

'My friends, today I have something to give to you. A present from Swami. Is it a little, little present? Oh no. Swami is feeling very kind. He is going to give each one of you a present that is very, very valuable. It is a present that he knew he was going to give long, long ago when he was meditating in the Himalayas and an inner command came to him that said: Go West, young man, go West. Yes, Swami is going to give you now—a future. It will be a future guarded more wisely than your future ever could be by any insurance company however big, however careful. Yes, I am giving it . . .'

Ghote slipped into a state of half-listening. The fellow's approach was not much different after all, he thought, from that of those holy men who had chanced to pass through his village when he was a boy and had brought everyone out to enjoy a distraction in their unvarying common round. Except that here the words were in English, and the promises were bigger.

But what about these people here listening? Were they as pleased as everybody in the village had been?

Seen from where he was now, face-on instead of from the back, they looked despite their orange clothes a good deal less like worshippers in a temple. To begin with they were, of course, almost all Westerners. The faces gazing up at Swami, for all that they bore a repeated and repeated expression of unthinking, undemanding happiness, were white or pink or ruddy red, not brown.

For a moment he hoped that he would be able to find only one brown face among them all, Nirmala Shahani's. But a longer look showed him there were quite a few Indians· present. There were in fact a good many of his compatriots in California, he recalled. He had read that in some magazine or other.

So not so easy to find Nirmala. It would have to be done methodically, in the manner recommended by Dr Hans Gross. Start at the nearer end of the first row, work your way all along it at an even, unhurrying speed, then go back to the start of the second row and repeat the process.

Mechanically his eyes swept past white face after white face. That fat sixty-year-old woman sitting on her little 'meditation bench', what had brought her all the way out here from the city to which with her soft, ring-glittering hands she obviously belonged? What was keeping her here was easy enough to see. Adoration for Swami. It shone from every inch of her lightly wrinkled cheeks and pursed lips.

But she was not the object of his quest. Move on. The next face, the next.

At last he came across a girl who might well be Nirmala. She was clearly an Indian and had the right complexion for a Sindhi like her father. She was about the right age, too, fresh-skinned with a small soft nose and big dark eyes. Eyes that were fixed on Swami with all the devotion of a puppy's.

But he ought to check the rest of the audience. He resumed his methodical survey. From just above him Swami's voice, gentle, persuasive, coaxing, drifted on.

'... Ah, I hear you. Swami hears what you are thinking in your heads only. You are saying: But now Swami has contradicted himself. He is no good at all this fellow, you are saying. Just now he told us the very opposite of what he said ten minutes ago. Oh, oh, my friends. Of course I am contradicting myself. I am contradicting

61

myself because the two things I have told you are like the two wings of a bird only. If a bird had one wing and no more, how can it fly, fly in the air like your souls too must fly? How can it? But if . . .'

With a sigh Ghote came to the end of another row of fixed, bemused, unthinking, utterly content faces.

Swami had power, he reflected. More power even than that which his own unthrobbing head still demonstrated.

In the middle of the next row there was another possible Indian girl, but though she was much the right age for Nirmala she appeared to be with a middle-aged couple who might well be her parents, a fat woman in a light pink sari wearing large horn-rimmed spectacles and a small dried-up man in tweed jacket and grey flannel trousers.

Then, a little further along, he spotted the first face he had seen that was not evidently under Swami's thrall. It belonged to an American girl. Young. Not much more than twenty, he guessed. And her complexion, unlike that of every other girl he had seen in California so far, did not radiate sheer well-being. Instead it was a dull white, and there was a tight, unrelenting frown on her forehead.

Because almost all American girls looked alike to him, he made a mental note of the clothes this one was wearing, blue jeans and a white high-necked pullover which looked—his eyesight seemed unusually keen after the Swami's lightning cure—decidedly grubby. Why on this warmly sunny Californian afternoon did she feel the need of a pullover? Yes, here was someone it might be a good idea to talk to if the Swami put up any opposition to Nirmala's departure. And that he was almost certain to do.

The Swami was telling a story now, about what a millionaire here in California who was also far advanced along the spiritual path had been able to do. It was only from something in the expressions of the next row of intent faces that Ghote had realized that the discourse had moved on to this. At first he had not been able to pinpoint the change. Then suddenly he had recognized a repeated look of bright-eyed expectation. He had seen just the same expression in the past on the face of his own little Ved when the boy had been listening to his mother telling him one of the old, old tales from the Ramayana. It showed complete abandonment to the unfolding story, marvellous to see in a child. But surely not somehow altogether right for adult face after adult face?

A chuckle of laughter that moved over the sea of upturned countenances like gentle wave greeted the end of the story. Ghote, proceeding systematically with his hunt for possible Nirmala Shahanis, noted that the man had clearly linked great wealth and high spirituality.

63

Was this a way of hinting to those members of his audience with money, like the fat lady with the glittering rings near the front, that gifts were acceptable? Was it a confidence man's softening-up?

Just at the beginning of the next row that he examined he found a face that looked as if it belonged to another dissenter. It was a girl's, but unlike the girl with the grubby white pullover this one was a picture of supreme Californian healthiness. Ghote saw her, for all that she was sitting cross-legged on the floor, as a tennis-player, a tireless tennis-player on one of the high mesh-walled courts he had seen as they had come out of Los Angeles. And she would be a player set to win.

He made a mental note of her clothes, a pale orange T-shirt and a white skirt. But he thought somehow that he would have no difficulty in recognizing her again, even in a crowd of other Californian goddesses. She would be the one more full of life, more confident than any of the others.

He went back to his searching. And only three faces further along he saw the most likely candidate yet for Nirmala Shahani. She was the right age and she had the right colour of skin for a Sindhi girl and even more than any of the other devotees, if that were possible, she seemed absolutely under the spell of Swami's words. As he watched her chubby, rounded, vacant-looking face he could see each of Swami's phrases reflected there as if a dim mirror was catching at a distance the brightness and the changing colours of a rippling display of lights.

He moved on to the other faces in the row, to the next row and the next until he had satisfied himself that he had examined every person in the hall. And all the while Swami's voice poured out from just above him. It was a stream, an unendingly flowing stream. From time to time there were little eddies in it, tiny back-currents, a joke, a long-held pause before a particularly striking declaration—'I shall go down in history with Henry Ford'—but the flow underneath was all the time rolling, rolling, rolling towards some distant sea, now faster a little, now slower, now tumbling playfully, now sliding swiftly and strongly.

Ghote, as he returned his gaze to the chubby, rather vacant face he was now sure belonged to Nirmala Shahani, half took in references to the silence within, to floating fragrances, to the soul, to the higher self, to gardens, to electricity, to being in tune with the infinite, to chickens wandering headless, to the elephant that breathed only ten times a minute and lived long, to the harmony that spread above and beyond everything. Each shift of meaning in the flowing stream, he saw, was reflected at once on the face of the hypnotized girl.

Yes, Nirmala Shahani.

65

Could he leave his place here at Swami's feet and get over to her? No. Not only would Swami plainly be aware if he moved so much as an inch but every other eye in the hall would see him too, seated as he was so close to the centre of their beaming, mindless, logic-and-shoes-abandoned devotion.

He would just have to wait till at last the discourse came to an end and then move quickly to get at the girl before any of her protectors realized what was happening.

But would Swami, Swami who had seen across the whole width of the hall the thudding inside his head, know at once what he was doing and somehow prevent him? It would be possible. A true yogi would possess that much power.

Yet was Swami a true yogi? Or was he simply a very cunning trickster? There were not only yogis back in India, there were clever conjurers too, the wandering magicians, the bhaghats, who made their way from village to village, from town to town, from fair to fair, mystifying all comers with their sleight-of-hand and their inherited knowledge of crowd psychology.

There was their famous mango-tree trick that had deceived plenty of sceptical, scientifically-minded Westerners. The mango stone handed round to the audience and carefully examined. Its ceremonial planting in a small pot of earth. A cloth whisked across the surface and, behold,

66

already the stone had sprouted. The cloth whisked again and there was a tiny plant. Another pass and another and the plant was big enough to have a minute mango beginning to form on it.

He had got to the bottom of that one himself once in his early days with the CID. The time he had watched such a performance among a wide-eyed crowd of Bombayites on the dusty grass of the Azad Maidan, had waited till they had dispersed, leaving at the bhaghat's feet not a few silver-grey paise coins, and had then sprung his police identity on the fellow. Just a little bullying and there had been produced for him the mussel-shell that, already buried in the earth of the pot next to where the mango stone was to be planted, could at an adroit flick of a finger as the cloth was waved above it release the little bendy sprout it contained. And then, once a degree of belief had been created, there were the succeeding larger mango sprigs that were concealed in the folds of the fellow's dhoti to be deftly inserted in the pot at the right moments.

Yes, sheer cleverness could achieve things that would astonish almost anybody. After all, when he himself had come into the hall when everyone else was already seated it was more than likely that Swami had noted his arrival. And then a few minutes of careful observation while that Westerner on the other side of the platform was playing his sitar, and it might well have been possible to deduce from the lines on his forehead and round his eyes that he was suffering from a severe headache. Yes, that was possible. Quite possible.

Suddenly then, just as he was trying to judge between the two explanations, from somewhere underneath Swami's silken orange upper garment there came a wheezy, high-pitched sound. It was a little tune. Its title scratched at the back of Ghote's mind. Yes. Surely. The Star-Spangled Banner.

The moment it had begun Swami had stopped speaking. His face in its frame of black-curling locks was lit by a broad smile. One or two people in the front of the audience began to titter with laughter and nudge each other. Swami held up his right arm so that the broad sleeve fell back. Round his wrist was a wide steel watchstrap and from the watch the little wheezy tune was coming.

'You see,' he said pointing with the finger of his other hand at the watch, 'my little alarm, so kindly given to me by our friend, Mrs Russell Walters. It tells me it is time for Swami to shut up. It tells me it is time for us to sing. Will you take your sitar and play Guru Nanak's wonderful song *O God Beautiful* for us, Johnananda?'

Johnananda. Johnananda, Ghote thought with a spurt of scorn. What a name. What a nonsensical mixture of West and East. That

68

English John with coupled on the Ananda which many swamis added to their name to signify Bliss. It was like yoking up together a motorcycle and a bullock. No, anyone with a name like that was a fake. No doubt about that. And if this sitar-playing Johnananda was a fake so surely was Swami.

And that meant that Nirmala Shahani was being kept here by some trickery with the object of getting hold through her of as much as possible of the wealth of Shahani Enterprises.

He looked across at the girl's plump, vacant face. She had switched her attention from Swami to Johnananda sending a few preliminary silvery cascades of sound out into the hall from his sitar. Well, perhaps if she could switch from Swami to that fellow, then she could be induced to change her loyalties back to her father once again without too much difficulty.

If only it was possible to get across there and start talking to her. But, plainly, there was no question still of doing that. No one in the audience had moved. Perhaps the best thing to do would be to wait till this meeting was over, let the girl get out of the hall and out of Swami's sight and then catch up with her.

He began measuring the distance between first the girl and the doors and then himself and the doors. If he waited till all the people between him and them had gone out, would his shoes still be where he had left them ready to slip into?

69

The devotees had begun singing now, a waft of sound rising up to the pure white dome of the roof above.

'O God beautiful, O God beautiful
In the forest Thou art green
In the mountain Thou art high
In the river—'

'You must sing also. Come, it is very easy. And the words are so beautiful. Sing. Sing.'

Swami was leaning down over him, his eyes exuding benevolence.

He felt a rush of fury. Yet it was somehow, too, slidingly easy to obey that sweet, intense voice.

The song began again without pause and he found he had joined in.

'In the mountain Thou art high
In the river Thou art restless...'

But he contrived to keep one corner of his mind concentrated on the girl Nirmala and on what he was going to do the moment he was free.

He saw, too, that Swami had moved away after issuing his invitation, or command, to him to join in. He had gone to the middle of the platform where on a broad orange sheet a tiger-skin had been laid. Seated on this, with back upright as a pole and bare feet protruding from his silken garments, he was adding a powerful sweet voice to the ocean-swell coming from below.

'In the forest Thou art green,
In the mountain . . .'

Again and again the words came round. On the platform Swami sang as if he was on some pinnacle of blind happiness. Down below his disciples sang back, as bemused, as faraway.

Were they never going to stop, Ghote thought as his lips, too, mindlessly repeated the simple words. Were they going to sit there lost in their singing till they all fell down from exhaustion? Did they never get anything done here? How would the world work if everybody was like this?

He shut his mouth with a snap.

And, as if that had been a signal, behind him on the platform Swami's high, sweet voice also abruptly ceased. And down below the chanting voices swiftly petered out into silence.

Arre, was the man going to subject him to a public rebuke for not going on and on with that song?

But no.

'Good, good,' came that sweet voice from the tigerskin. 'That was very good. And later perhaps we will sing again. Or we will have a

71

hum. But now you have things that you want to ask Swami. When he talks sometimes he forgets to make everything quite, quite simple. So now you can ask me questions. Any question you like.'

Would this be the time to move so as to be ready to pounce on Nirmala Shahani as soon as she had taken herself out of Swami's influence? But no one in the audience got up from the floor and Ghote resigned himself to a longer wait.

'Swamiji,' an American girl's voice piped up from somewhere near the front of the circular floor. 'Swamiji, have you ever brought a person back to life when they were dead?'

Swami gave a little coy chuckle.

'Oh, such questions she asks. But I will tell you the true answer. No. No, I have not restored any dead person to life. Yet.'

A murmur of wonder at the feat-to-come rippled through the seated devotees. Then a tall young man got to his feet from where he had been seated in the first row, not on any clever little stool or squabby cushion, Ghote noted, but on the floor itself. He had a long, lean face, fixed and intent as if it were carved.

'Swamiji,' he said, his voice harsh with anxiety, 'I have this problem. I've got to get rid of the greed I feel within. I really want this. And I've meditated for it, and, well, I guess I've done everything you've ever told us to do. But it's still there, Swamiji, the greed. I can feel it like a

72

little hard lump inside of me. So what do I do next, Swamiji? Please, what do I do?'

From a snicker of unease that seemed to zigzag through at least some part of Swami's audience Ghote deduced that the young man's earnest questioning had found an echo in some at least of the orange-clad disciples.

He turned his head to watch Swami as he answered. How would he deal with something that, however humbly expressed, was in fact a challenge?

Swami smiled.

It was a smile yet fuller, yet sweeter, than any he had bestowed on them before. Then with the plump forefinger of his extended, palm-up left hand he made a little beckoning gesture, so insignificant that he might have been doing no more than nudge nearer himself some unimportant little object.

But the lanky, long-faced questioner moved towards the platform and on to it as if he was being drawn there by a smooth nylon rope reeled in by a steadily thrumming electric motor.

There was a hushed silence throughout the whole white-domed hall as he came to a halt just in front of Swami's tiger-skin.

'You must kneel,' Swami said, still smiling and smiling.

The tall young man thumped down to his knees. His long, intent face was little more than a foot away from Swami's lusciously-locked, full-smiling one.

For a full minute, though it seemed to Ghote much longer, Swami looked deep into the lean, young face in front of him. From where he was sitting Ghote had only an oblique view of Swami's eyes, but even so he distinctly felt that they possessed a hypnotic pull.

Then at last Swami spoke, his voice low and honeyed but clear to hear in the tense silence.

'Why didn't you come before?'

The young man's Adam apple rose and fell in his thin, almost child-like neck.

'I—I guess I thought it wouldn't be right to—to trouble you, Swamiji.'

'No,' said that low, clear voice. 'That was not the reason. It was pride. Too much pride. A heart full of pride.'

The kneeling young man bent his head.

And suddenly, Ghote saw, on Swami's gentle face there had appeared a look of anger. Of formidable anger.

'Why don't you become a human being?' the voice, honey no longer, stormed at the young man. 'Why not? Why do you go on like this? Stop it. Stop. Throw it away. Be human. Be a human being.'

The words were commands. And criticism. Unsparing criticism.

Ghote, new to it all, felt their sting almost as if they had been directed at himself.

What are they feeling down there, the others, he thought. The ones who have been here for weeks or months. They must be dominated. Held as slaves.

And from this man with all this power he had to wrest Nirmala Shahani.

His mouth went dry.

The young American on the platform was trying to give Swami an answer. But whatever justification of himself he was attempting to produce emerged only as a mumble.

Swami cut into the confused syllables like a blade.

'Why?' he stormed. 'Why? Why? Why? I ask: why haven't you made yourself a human being?'

'I can't.'

The cry was tugged from the boy as if it had been wrenched from his inner flesh.

And it was at once answered. By a slap. A ringing slap delivered with the full force of Swami's right arm clean on to the side of the boy's face.

By a slap and then another. And another, and another. The sound of them cracked into the still air under the wide white dome of the hall. The first had brought from the seated devotees a tiny, suppressed gasp of dismay. But each one after was received in silence.

It is the silence, Ghote thought, of abject acceptance. Of the whipped dog.

Yet, he wondered, are there just possibly one

75

or two minds out there that do not accept all this? The girl in the grubby white pullover with that fixed frown on her muddy-complexioned face? That other girl, the radiantly healthy tennis-player?

But if either of them was protesting at this scene, she was doing so inwardly. There was not a murmur anywhere in the whole of the big hall.

'Go now,' Swami said to the boy at last. 'Go, and do not come back to me until you are ready for me to see you.'

The kneeling boy turned his body away and actually crawled to the side of the platform before getting to his feet and circling the wide hall with his face held the whole time looking at the pure white wall beside him until at last he slipped out through the double doors.

'But nobody is sitting near Swami.'

That voice was all honey again. Coy honey.

'Come. Come up and sit by Swami. Swami likes to have his friends near him. Come. Come up. Mrs Russell Walters, you must come and sit close to Swami.'

Ghote saw the fat woman with the rings push herself up from her meditation stool that ingeniously gave her the appearance of sitting on the floor. Of course, he thought, she is the one who gave Swami that very expensive watch.

He watched her go wobblingly up the steps on to the platform and then, with a giggle that struck him as being altogether unseemly, stoop

76

and touch Swami's feet before she settled down on the floor within a few inches of his tiger-skin. Half-a-dozen other disciples who apparently knew they were equally privileged had followed her on to the platform, touched Swami's feet in their turn and had placed themselves at varying distances from him. The last of them, coming forward only after a short gap, was the tennis-player girl. After she had stooped, rather more quickly than the others, to touch Swami's bare toes she positioned herself almost directly behind him, pulled a secretary's note-pad out of a leather bag she had slung on her shoulder and propped it open on her knee as she sat cross-legged.

So close to the fellow, Ghote thought. So close, and yet not totally under his influence. Perhaps here was something...

'Swamiji,' Mrs Russell Walters said in a voice that must have been too quiet to reach the body of the disciples still seated on the floor of the hall but which Ghote, straining a little, could make out quite clearly. 'Swamiji, have you been thinking now about what I asked you last week?'

Swami made a brushing-away gesture with his two plump hands.

'No, no, no, no,' he said. 'You must not be mentioning such things, Mrs Russell Walters.'

'Oh, but I must. I am. Swamiji, have you made up your mind which one it is to be?'

Swami gave her a beaming smile, such as a

77

doting uncle might give to a two-year old.

'You know Swami cannot make up his mind,' he said. 'You know he doesn't understand anything about such things.'

Mrs Russell Walters returned his smile with a little nod of determination that sent her several chins wobbling this way and that.

'Well, if your mind's not made up,' she said, 'mine is. I'm going to go right ahead and get you what I think is best myself.'
Ghote felt a little spurt of elation.

So she was going to get something more for Swami, this wealthy woman who had already given him a wristwatch that any film star in Bombay would be proud to show off. Here was proof, if anything was, that the fellow was on the make here in money-oozing California.

He inclined his head at a slightly changed angle so as to be sure of catching every next word of the conversation up on the platform.

'Oh, Mrs Russell Walters, Mrs Russell Walters, you are a very naughty lady. You are spoiling poor Swami.'

'Yes, and I mean to go right on doing just that. Now, am I going to have to do the choosing, or will you tell me?'

'But how should I know which is best? My head is always so full of fine thoughts. It is thinking of flowers and of the path to God, not of motor-cars only.'

Motor-cars. So Mrs Russell Walters was

going to give Swami a car. And—he had said it himself—whichever one was the best. The best out of all those huge, wide, splendid, gleaming machines they had walked past in the car-park at the airport. The best of them. This was certainly not how a real yogi should behave.

And abruptly Ghote realized that his feelings about the fellow were being shared. By the tennis-player girl with the note-pad on her knee. On her face that, as she had stooped to touch Swami's feet, had worn a bursting-with-health, white-teethed, oral-hygiene-programme smile there was now a look of dismay. Of deep dismay, that she was fighting to keep back.

As soon as he could he must have a quiet word with that girl.

It was as he made this resolution that he became aware that he had seen something else as well. Swami's toes. While the fellow had been telling Mrs Russell Walters that his head was full of fine thoughts instead of thoughts about cars his toes had suddenly tightly curled up.

Curled-up toes were a sign that, in his everyday work among Bombay's criminals, he had long ago learned to look out for. It was one of the tricks of his trade. As often as not when someone was telling a lie their feet betrayed them. The toes curled up. So, like all his colleagues, he had learnt always to place himself where he could see a suspect's bare or sandalled feet.

So, yes, beyond doubt Swami was no more than—

From the back of the hall there came a single loud crash, heart-thumpingly sudden in the atmosphere of quiet devotion.

Ghote's eyes zoomed to the entrance doors.

There, enormous, towering, stood the huge, belly-jutting figure of Fred Hoskins. Between his two out-thrust hands, menacingly held, was his piece. His gun.

CHAPTER FIVE

It was as if a fanning-out jet of fiercely rushing water had spewed from the doors. Disciple after disciple, a moment earlier sitting cross-legged and straight-backed, wholly turned in loving bemusement towards Swami up on the platform, had toppled over to lie on the floor like so many plastic traffic bollards swept down by some fireman's hose.

There was no sound other than the thump-thump-thump of bodies, young and old, skinny and fat, hitting the floor with unaccustomed force.

What to do, Ghote asked himself. Call over to Fred Hoskins and say that back-up—was that the word?—was not needed? Or keep quiet and not give away that he himself was here with the

80

fellow?

His dilemma was solved for him in a way he had not at all expected.

From among the bodies on the floor a voice spoke. A girl's voice with a husky full-throatedness that Ghote at once recognized as being the English of a well-off Indian.

'Oh, it is Mr Hoskins. Mr Hoskins, what are you doing here again? And what for have you got that gun?'

Lithely to her feet there rose from the welter of disciples not the chubby, vacant-faced girl Ghote had settled on as being Nirmala Shahani but the girl he had first noted as a possible, the one with the big dark eyes and small soft nose. With quiet confidence she set out towards the jutting-bellied, jackal-haired private eye, standing with his gun still thrust aggressively forward in his two clasped hands.

Ghote decided he could no longer pose as a mere chance visitor. He must get hold of Nirmala Shahani as quickly as he could.

He ran, dodging his way between the stranded seal-like forms of the still crouching disciples, and before she had reached Fred Hoskins he succeeded in getting to her.

'Excuse me, please,' he said, catching her by the elbow. 'I must speak with you. My name is Ghote. I have been sent by your father.'

Would these few words alone do the trick? Would the sudden knowledge thrust on the girl

81

that her father had sent someone all the way to California for her be enough to break the spell she was held in?

She turned.

His first thought, seeing her close-to, was how pretty she was. She was all that an Indian girl ought to be. Big brown eyes, sparkling darkly with instant interest in everything around her. Meltingly soft flesh, vulnerably in need of being protected. And that little, soft nose, like that of some new-born animal, a baby deer or floppy-legged puppy, at once absurdly inquisitive and appallingly at the mercy of the brutal facts of the world.

If I had a daughter myself, he thought before he could stop himself, this is the girl I would like her to be.

But it was no submissive Hindu daughter who answered his shock-treatment introduction.

'My father? What for is he wanting to interfere? Was he told what I had said to Mr Hoskins? Yes, if he sent you he must have been. So why is he sending you at all?'

Ghote saw that her sharp questions were attracting the attention of the disciples near them, beginning now cautiously to get to their feet as Fred Hoskins slowly lowered his gun. For all their allegiance to things spiritual, plain curiosity seemed to be dominant in a good many of them.

'Can we go outside to talk?' he said to

Nirmala.

'What is there to talk?'

But he put a hand firmly on to her elbow and a slight pressure was enough to propel her towards the double doors and out into the shoe-crowded lobby with Fred Hoskins going ahead of them stuffing the gun back into the broad leather belt over which his grain-sack belly protruded.

'Mr Hosk—Fred,' Ghote said. 'Please will you return to your car wherever you have put it? We may need to make a very, very rapid getaway.'

He felt pleased at the ruse he had hit on, and particularly with that word getaway. That was really American. And the ruse worked, too.

'Inspector, since you are a DV, which is the term we employ for Distinguished Visitor,' Fred Hoskins said, 'I am happy to place my vehicle at your complete disposal.'

He brought a big beef-red hand up to his short jackal-fur crown of hair, turned and crashed through the double doors out of the building.

Ghote faced Nirmala Shahani once more.

'Miss Shahani,' he said, 'I would very much like to make certain that you understand exactly what it is that your father is wanting.'

'He is wanting me to leave the ashram,' the girl shot back in answer. 'And I am not going to go. Not, not, not. Swami will never say that I

83

must go.'

'But it is not Swami who should say,' Ghote replied, upset by this fierceness shown by someone who ought, he felt, to be gentle and willing. 'Miss Shahani, you depend on your father. And your father is requesting you to return to Bombay.'

Nirmal Shahani straightened her back.

'I do not depend on Daddyji,' she said. 'I do not depend on him any more. I am depending on Swami only.'

'But what are you going to live on? Your father told me that you have no money left in your joint account at the State Bank of India, at Wilshire—'

'Yes, yes. There is none, none. I have given it all to Swami. What for am I needing money? I have Swami's love. Swami's love will look after me always.'

'You have given him all your money? Every rupee? Every dollar?'

'Yes. Yes, yes. And I would have given more if there had been more in the account. I would give anything to Swami.'

For a moment Ghote was at a loss for words. What could he say that would penetrate the layer of innocence that Nirmala had wrapped round herself? That protective fluff of down?

But there was one possible thing. He tried it.

'You are not the only one who gives to Swami, Miss Shahani.'

'No. All give. All long to give. We love Swami.'

'But some give very, very much more than others,' Ghote said. 'And Swami makes those people his special favourites.'

'What special favourites? Swami loves us all. If somebody is needing his special attention, then they are getting. That is all.'

'They get Swami's special attention,' Ghote echoed. 'They? Is it a he who gets it, or a she?'

'He or she. What does it matter? Do you think Swami notices whether he is loving a boy or a girl only?'

'Perhaps he does not. But perhaps he does notice whether he is giving his special favour to a girl who has no more to give him or to a rich, rich American lady who can give and give and give again. Give a wristwatch with a special alarm that plays a tune one week and next week gives a motor-car.'

'Mrs Russell Walters?' Nirmala asked, and there was a hint of alarm in her voice.

So that fluff of innocence can be penetrated perhaps, Ghote thought.

'Mrs Russell Walters is going to give Swami a motor-car,' he stated flatly.

'Why such a *hungama* over that?' Nirmala answered, with a quick, proud upward tilt of her soft little nose. 'What does Swami care if he had a thousand motor-cars or none? She is just giving so that he can go from place to place more

85

quickly telling everybody what a wonderful future is waiting for them.'

'But perhaps Swami does care about cars,' Ghote replied, suddenly acutely conscious of how he was treading on a thin mud-crust over a deep-sucking, unknown swamp. 'Perhaps Swami cares very much about just what sort of a car Mrs Russell Walters would give.'

Nirmala laughed.

'Swamiji does not know one car from another,' she said. 'He is far above all motor-cars.'

For an instant Ghote held back. Then he plunged.

'What if I could prove to you that Swami does know just that?' he said. 'What if I could prove that he knew already that Mrs Russell Walters wants to give him a car and that he has spent many hours thinking about just which great big American model would be best? If I could do that, would you still think he cared nothing for money?'

'You would not prove,' Nirmala answered.

'But if I did...?'

Nirmala gave a scornful toss of her head.

'If you can prove-prove to me that Swami knows even one car from another,' she said, 'then I will take the next flight back to Bombay.'

'Very good,' Ghote said, trying to hide his inner dismay at what he had pledged himself to do. 'Where shall I be able to find you when I am ready?'

'I stay in the hut they are calling Shanti Sadan. Ask anybody.'

'Then I will see you before very long.'

He turned away.

What had he done? Was there something in the air of California that made everybody behave as if they were twice as large as life? Had whatever it was that made people here do things like buy cars that were more like battleships already entered into him?

To tell Nirmala he could prove Swami knew about the different models of cars in America: it was nothing more than a gigantic bluff. What had he had to go on? Just the fellow's curled-up toes. Even if it had been a direct lie assuring Mrs Russell Walters he knew nothing about cars, how was that to be proved?

And if he failed in that, then Nirmala was going to be more determined than ever to stay here. To stay in the clutches of a man who was nothing but a trickster.

Except that he himself had no headache.

And, if Swami was not a trickster but a true yogi, what then? If Swami was like a yogi back in Bombay years ago whom they had arrested, wrongly as it turned out, and who had been found each morning sitting calmly outside the cell he had been locked up in the previous night, then surely he would be after all a very good person to have charge of a young girl.

87

But to go back to Bombay and to tell Ranjee Shahani that: there would be fireworks then all right. The Minister would get to hear in no time at all. And then there would be a posting for him. To some little town far out in the mofussil where nothing ever happened, to waste out the rest of his days.

Still, there was one thing he could do. One tiny chance open to him.

He pushed wide the doors and went back into the hall.

There had been two points he had noticed while Mrs Russell Walters had been trying to persuade Swami to have a big, new car. There had been Swami's curling toes. But there had also been the look on the face of the tennis-player girl. The look of deeply hurt dismay that had drained the bursting-with-health radiance out of her.

He had promised himself the moment before Fred Hoskins had come crashing in at the doors with his piece that he would have a quiet word with that girl at some time. Now he could not wait.

He saw that the disturbance caused by the private-eye's unexpected entrance had apparently brought the meeting to an end sooner than intended. The Swami had left and disciples, in flowing garments in every shade of orange, in T-shirts, in blue jeans, a good many carrying babies, others linked arm in arm, were already beginning to make their way towards the door.

He pushed through them with a determination that he knew was out of keeping with the general atmosphere of hazy benevolence. And which gave him an inward jab of sharp pleasure.

The Western sitar-player, Johnananda, seemed to be making an announcement standing up on the platform, his voice rising desperately above the buzz of talk as the disciples swirled towards the doors. To Ghote's surprise his accent was not darkly American but British. A screechy British bray.

'Before you go... Before you go... Chaps... Girls... Before you go, one thing. Remember tonight is special. Very, very special. It's tonight that Swamiji is going to meditate in here all night. In the morning he's going to have a very special announcement to make to everybody. Chaps... Girls...'

Despite his urgency nobody was paying much attention. Ghote's opinion of the fellow fell yet further. An Englishman, but not even a born-to-rule one such as he had known from a distance in his boyhood. No, no amount of sitar-playing and head-shaving could disguise his being a fake.

'So no-one—Please. Please. No one is to come in here after six o'clock tonight. Swamiji will come out at six tomorrow morning, and I want

89

you all . . . It would be very nice if everyone was outside to greet him.'

The hall was fast emptying. But up on the platform the girl with the note-pad was standing, looking as if she was waiting for everyone else to go. As if she could not wait to be alone.

Ghote went up on to the platform and crossed over to her.

'Good afternoon, madam,' he said. 'I am thinking that you can be of very, very much assistance to me.'

The oral-hygiene smile appeared on the girl's face. But, Ghote thought, it had been a hard struggle to put it there.

'What can I do for you, friend?'

'Well, I was seeing you just now with your note-pad sitting close to Swami, and I thought that you were perhaps his personal assistant also.'

'Yeah, that's right. Only Swami doesn't think of me as—'

For an instant she hesitated.

'Well,' she went on almost at once, 'I was about to say that Swami doesn't believe in any of that personal-assistant, power-structure stuff. I'm his plain secretary, if anything. I mean, he just found out one day I had pretty good shorthand and he asked if I would sit by him and take notes of everything he said. He's writing a book, you know.'

'Oh, yes? That is very good. What is it to be about, please?'

'About? Why, about him, of course. It'll be his thoughts and his sayings and all. He says one day it'll be read all over the world, and it'll tell millions of people the way they ought to live.'

The longer she went on about it, Ghote thought, the less she seemed to believe what she was saying.

'Please,' he asked, 'I would be very glad to be knowing your name, madam.'

'It's Emily.'

'Emily. I see.' He allowed a small barb of irritation to surface. 'It is Emily only?'

'No. No, I guess. Emily Kanin, if you want to know. But we don't go for all that formality at the ashram. Just call me Emily.'

'Very good. Emily. Yes. Well, please, Emily, I was wanting to know if I could have an interview with Swami. There is a very, very important matter I am wishing to put to him.'

He hoped, violently, that Emily would not say that, yes, he could see Swami straight away. The thought of trying to wrest Nirmala Shahani from him in a direct confrontation was almost too much for him. But he had to keep Emily talking about Swami, and asking for an interview had been the best way to do so that he could think of.

'I guess Swami hasn't got a free minute before six o'clock,' Emily answered, to his relief. 'And,

91

you may not know, but he's going into an all-night meditation then. He's got a terrific problem he wants to solve.'

'Oh, I see. I see. And he is always solving his problems by meditating only?'

'He certainly is. But you're Indian, aren't you? You ought to know what can be done by meditating.'

'Well, not every Indian is very, very spiritual, you know.'

Ghote thought briefly of Nirmala Shahani's father in his huge luxurious office.

'But, please,' he added quickly, 'what is this problem that Swami is facing?'

'I'm afraid I just can't tell you. I don't even have an idea myself, as a matter of fact. All kinds of things could be worrying him. His book. Or maybe the way some of the guys and girls here are behaving. Finances. Anything. The ashram costs a heck of a lot to run, you know.'

'Oh, yes, I suppose that must be so. Who owns all the magnificent land it is on, please? Does the ashram go all the way down to the gate at the road?'

'Yeah.'

She gave a sudden little frown.

'It's all in Swami's name actually,' she said, speaking slowly, her mind plainly elsewhere. 'He was given most of it. He needed somewhere to start the ashram. So he meditated, and

92

someone came up with an unexpected gift.'

Ghote did his best to look extremely impressed.

'Then Swami must be a very, very rich man?' he asked.

'Yeah. Well, technically. I suppose. But technically only, you understand. The ashram really belongs to God. Or—'

For the second time Emily, the radiantly healthy, the tennis-player, hesitated. Then she went on in a rush.

'Yeah, the ashram belongs to God. But of course it had to be in someone's name. For tax purposes, you know. The IRS—that's our Internal Revenue Service—just need a name on their tax-forms. So Swami said it might as well be his name as anybody else's. That's what Swami said.'

Ghote thought he could detect a note of defiance in these last words. Of defiance against certain inner thoughts the girl must have.

He decided to press forward.

'And all these gifts Swami is getting?' he asked. 'Like—Like that wristwatch he was showing. Are they in his name also while they belong truly to God, or are they for him himself?'

Emily looked even more uneasy.

'That's hard to say,' she answered eventually. 'I mean, well, something like a watch... Well, that's something that's only useful to the person who wears it, isn't it? It'd only make sense for it to be his alone.'

'And a car also?'

Had he gone too far? Was it a mistake to have let this girl, who for all the doubts he suspected she had must be close indeed to Swami, learn that he had overheard that quiet conversation up on the platform?

But at once the look on Emily's face told him that he need not fear her giving him away. The single word car had hit her like a blow on the bridge of the nose.

'I—I don't know,' she stammered. 'I thought—I used to think...'

'Swami very much wants a big, big car, isn't it?' Ghote jumped in. 'When he was saying to that lady, to Mrs Russell Walters, that he was knowing nothing about cars at all, that was not true, was it? Swami does know about cars. He has been finding out which is the best of them all after Mrs Russell Walters was saying she would get him one. Isn't it? Isn't it?'

'Yes,' said Emily.

It was the merest whisper of a word.

'That was something you did not want to hear, what Swami said up here with Mrs Russell Walters?' Ghote said. 'Up to then you had still believed in Swami, isn't it?'

'Yes. Yes, I came here—'

She checked herself.

'Oh, how's anybody to know?' she said. 'I

94

guess Swami needs a car. And if he's going to ask for one with quadrophonic speakers in it, TV set, phone, CB radio, refrigerator, the very best you can buy, well, if he wants everything Mrs Russell Walters is ready to get for him, then...'

'But how does he know just what is the best car?' Ghote persisted. 'If he is going to tell Mrs Russell Walters just what he is wanting, how does he know which make to buy?'

'Brochures,' Emily answered simply. 'That's why I knew he was telling a downright lie. He'd asked me to get him all the brochures and the car magazines I could lay my hands on. He's got a whole pile of them in his own house, the place with the orange roof, you know. They're there right now.'

She sounded like someone who has run the hardest race of their life. And lost at the tape.

Ghote looked at her.

'Miss Emily,' he said, 'do not forget one thing.'

She gave him a quick glance, a sudden flicker of new hope.

'Do not forget this, Miss Emily. When I came into the hall here I had just been having a long, long air-journey all the way from Bombay. My head was beating and beating. And Swami took one look at me right across to near the doors over there, and he knew at once. He knew and he called to me, and then he put his hand on my

95

neck, Miss Emily, and the pain went. The pain went.'

'Yeah,' she said slowly. 'Yeah, it's true, isn't it? There is something else. There is more to this world than—Than, oh, business and cheating guys and tennis and boys and making some bucks and fixing yourself up with the best condo in the block. There is, isn't there?'

'Yes,' said Ghote. 'There is.'

CHAPTER SIX

It was almost midnight at the ashram. Inspector Ghote stood some hundred yards downhill from the circle of buildings at the heart of the place, his back to the harsh, flaky-barked trunk of a redwood tree, breathing in the cool odoriferous air. Above, the sky was pricked with an infinite quantity of stars, seemingly smaller, harder and more diamond-like than the familiar rich spangling of the Indian night.

Ahead all appeared to be profoundly quiet. The ashram's disciples in their huts and tents scattered through the forest were surely all blamelessly sleeping. And under the white dome of the Meditation Hall, palely visible against the distant sky, the Swami With No Name must be sitting, upright of back, feet tucked against the inner side of his thighs, soundlessly meditating

96

on his tiger-skin.

Or would he be?

Was he really a meditator? Or was he no more than a confidence trickster? A man not much different from a dozen clever criminals encountered over the years in Bombay, if perhaps as clever or more clever even, more ruthless even, than any of them?

For the umpteenth time Ghote debated it in his head. And came, once more, to the same conclusion. The Swami was a man who had developed in himself a power different from the everyday feelings, the lust for fame, money or influence that otherwise might motivate him. Yes, he was capable of truly meditating. He was capable of curing in an instant with a firm touch of his unnaturally warm hand a pounding headache.

So now, surely, he would be there in the Meditation Hall in that deep state of inner-directed striving they called *samadhi*. And there would therefore be nothing to prevent a person who lived in the ordinary world and who had enough determination from entering the fellow's extraordinary orange-roofed private house and making sure that there, ready to be shown to Nirmala Shahani as soon as he could get hold of her, was a solid pile of richly printed brochures and magazines detailing every last advantage of the best and most expensive automobiles to be found in the American market.

97

Ghote momentarily bit his lower lip. He was going to beat this fellow. He was going to wrest the girl he had been sent to rescue from his grasp and take her away to her rightful home.

He set off up the hill.

He felt alertly ready for the task he had set himself. He had had five hours of solid sleep in a nearby motel. Fred Hoskins had insisted on getting him a room with a waterbed but even the curious rolling motion underneath him had not, thanks to his extreme fatigue, succeeded in keeping him awake for even a few minutes. He had, too, eaten a good meal, a huge glass of fresh orange juice, machine-extracted in front of his eyes from oranges so large that he had not been able to prevent himself expecting to smell the sharp tang of grapefruit, with a plate of fried eggs, again so big that he had not liked to think of the chickens that could lay them. Even having to watch Fred Hoskins, seated opposite him, ravenously demolish a hardly-cooked steak so huge that it lolloped over the edges of the plate had not put him off.

And—he chuckled quietly to himself—he had succeeded in avoiding any unwanted assistance now by telling the jutting-bellied private-eye after the meal that he wanted to go back to that waterbed. He had even offered the opinion, in a major sacrifice of truthfulness, that the thing was a very great improvement on the rope-strung charpoy of India. And then he had

98

slipped out of the window of his room at the back of the motel and had briskly walked the four or five miles back to the ashram.

Just short of the inner circle he came to a halt again.

Swami's extraordinary, spiralling-roofed house was only some twenty yards distant and the big white dome of the Meditation Hall another twenty or thirty yards further on. There was still no sign of life anywhere. Not a light in any of the other buildings of the circle. Not a sound.

A few careful, careless questions to the disciple who had resumed his duties at the Visitors Centre on their way to the motel had elicited the information that Swami's house consisted in fact of no more than one large room under its orange roof, partitioned off at the back into a small bedroom and a small bathroom. The disciple had said proudly that Swami had designed the whole place himself in one long session of meditation. An architect called in to bring it to reality had declared that its high-spiralling, flyaway roof, conceived of as illustrating man's soaring soul, was impossible of construction. 'But we did it. We all just pitched in thinking of Swami and there it was.'

Ghote maintained his watch on the house for another full five minutes and then slowly and cautiously he approached the building and began to walk round it, peering hard in the dim light of the moonless night at its rough log walls, at the eaves of its roof above them. There seemed to be nothing to give him any cause for doubts. The logs were solidly set together, thick and substantial, and there was nothing else but them. Not a single window, not a ventilator, even at the back where presumably bathroom and bedroom were.

Then, with a suddenness that sent his heart beating and racing, he walked straight into something. His shin came into sharp contact with a metallic object and there was a jangle of sound.

In the still darkness it seemed so noisy that he expected in an instant voices would be raised everywhere, feet would come running.

He stood absolutely still.

And nothing happened. His heart slowed to its accustomed pace, and he realized that in fact the noise made by whatever it was he had stumbled on had not been very loud.

He peered downwards.

It was a bicycle. The bicycle he had looked at as he had walked through the passageway between Swami's house and the ashram dining-hall when he had first been going to the Meditation Hall. The ancient bicycle that had, because of the familiarity of its half-repaired state, given him at that moment a much-needed burst of confidence. He saw that it had in fact been moved a little from its original position.

Evidently whoever owned it had made one more attempt at repairing it—they seemed to have gone off with its damaged inner tube—and had left it sticking further out into the passageway.

Well, once more life's intractabilities seemed to have defeated someone. And, once more, paradoxically, this gave him a spurt of confidence.

Yes, all was well. No one was near and there was nothing to prevent him just going into this strange-looking building, seeing what he wanted to see and quietly leaving, ready as soon as he could find Nirmala Shahani's hut to prove his rash assertion to her about Swami's integrity. The two of them could be on a plane to Bombay together before the next day was out. Perhaps within a week even he himself would be in Banaras, with Protima beside him no longer bitterly accusing, listening to the words of some real swamis—and perhaps noting some he could confidently put down as fakes.

There would be no difficulty about getting into the house either, not if what the disciple at the Visitors Centre had said was true.

'We can always go right ahead and see Swamiji, you know. The doors of his house are never locked. No doors in the ashram have locks. We can just walk right in on Swami, only of course we never do.'

'No, no. Of course not. That would be quite wrong.'

It had been a little heartless to play up to the young enthusiast like that. But there was a task to be carried out.

He took one last look round. Under the cold glittering Californian stars all was hushedly still.

He marched over to the couple of steps leading up to the doors of the house, paused at the top and then gently pushed. With only the faintest of creaks the doors gave way in front of him.

A single quiet step and he was inside.

Once the doors were closed behind him he dared bring out the flashlight he had bought at the motel shop. Fred Hoskins had given him a tremendous lecturing when he had made out before going to bed that he was afraid the power supply at the place might fail but he had defied his scorn and made the purchase. By the flashlight beam he saw now that the young man at the Visitors Centre had a little misled him. Swami's house did not consist only of the one large room with a bedroom and bathroom at the back. He was still only in an entrance lobby, presumably a place where people coming in to see the great man could leave their shoes, and perhaps their logic too.

He stooped and removed his own shoes, placing them carefully just beside the open double doors, pointing outwards. The need for silence rather than respect, he thought with a hint of a smile. And no harm in putting them where he could scoop them up if he should have to leave in a hurry.

He could make out all of the lobby now, not that there was a great deal to see, just a small statue of the Dancing Nataraj on a tall pedestal and the single plain door that led into the interior of the building.

With minute care he turned the door-handle and exerted a little pressure. The door moved open easily. But the instant it began to do so he saw that the room on the far side was bright with light. The solid door had blotted it all out till now.

He took his hand away, extinguished his flashlight and left the door the merest quarter of an inch open. Was Swami here and not in the Meditation Hall after all?

As unmoving as the statue on its pillar beside him, he stood and thought.

Should he simply creep away? Or should he chance it on the supposition that Swami had simply left the lights on inside when he had gone out? Was the fellow meditating where he had said he would be, a true yogi despite the signs of greed he had shown over Mrs Russell Walters and her offer? Or was he lying asleep inside, in the far bedroom, a grin of triumph on his trickster's face?

He turned his head so that his ear was as near as he could get it to the crack at the edge of the door. Could he hear anything? Was there

103

anything to hear?

No. No, he was certain. There was nothing. Not even the faintest sound of breathing.

He decided suddenly to risk it. If Swami was there inside he could pretend that he had come to see him, that he was seeking guidance even, that he did not know the fellow was supposed to be elsewhere.

For a few extra seconds he continued to listen at the door-crack. But there was nothing. Not the slightest of moans, not a sigh.

He thrust the heavy door wide.

The Swami Without A Name, at once yogi and cunning cheat, was lying flat on his back in the centre of the large, almost bare room. His throat was cut from ear to ear.

Bare-chested with only a silken orange dhoti round his middle and the thick black cord of a sacred necklace across his ample, palely brown chest, he lay with his head seemingly tossed back and his thick curling black locks spread out round it on the bare polished boards of the floor. The blood from the gaping wound in his neck had collected in a small puddle beside him, and as Ghote stood there, shocked into immobility, suddenly its surface tension broke and a thin trickle ran out a few inches further over the close-boarded floor.

The sudden tiny shocking little event brought Ghote at once back to life. And to the instant of realization of what in fact that event meant.

If the blood was still liquid like that, the man must have been killed only minutes earlier. Not more than ten minutes at the most. Blood congealed at least that quickly: it was a fact he remembered from lectures in his days at Police College.

So Swami must have been alive still when he himself had gone prowling round the outside of this house. But then whoever had killed him— and there was no weapon here, he must have been killed by someone—must still be inside the house. They must be. During the time he had made his circuit of the building the area immediately in front of it had not been out of his sight for more than four or five seconds while he had walked past the back wall. No one could have come out and walked away without his seeing them. They could not.

Swiftly, in his socked feet, Ghote moved towards the two doors at the back of the big, bare room. The doors to Swami's bedroom and his bathroom. The killer must be behind one or the other of them.

But which?

Impossible to decide.

He gave the floor in front of each door a long, careful inspection under the bright glare of light that came from the four separate globes in the neatly wood-panelled ceiling. There was not the least sign to indicate that anyone had gone through one rather than the other, not a pineneedle off the bottom of a shoe, not a crumb of red earth.

And in the room itself—he looked back at it—there was nowhere where anybody could possibly be hiding. The sole piece of furniture was a sort of low throne against one of the bare walls, a mattress covered in yellow silk with some cushions on it. Besides that there was nothing, unless you counted an incongruous telephone on the floor beside the yellow-silk throne, a gleaming, all-white telephone. Otherwise everything was strikingly bare.

So into which little room at the back had the murderer gone? Into Swami's bedroom? Or his bathroom?

And which in fact was which? There was no telling. The two doors were identical, solid blanks of light-coloured wood like the door from the lobby.

There was nothing to choose between them. And yet behind one of them there must be standing the person who had murdered Swami. Armed with the very knife or dagger they had used. And ready, no doubt, to use it again. It must have been the faint creak which the outer doors had made when he had pushed them gently open that had alerted them. In the short time that he himself had been standing in the lobby, taking off his shoes and looking at the Dancing Nataraj on its pedestal and the oblong of the door in front of him, they must have

106

silently retreated into one of these two rooms.

But which? Which?

He must make up his mind one way or the other within the next few seconds. If he was to keep any vestige of surprise on his side—and, unarmed as he was, he would need all the surprise he could find if he was going to subdue whoever held that appallingly sharp knife—then every half-second ticking away counted.

He slid on socked feet towards the door on his left, shot out his left hand to its handle, paused for one heartbeat more and then in one swift continuing movement jerked it round and swung his right shoulder hard against the door.

It hurtled back.

And the room that confronted him—it was the bedroom, he saw a wide bed that was solid to the ground with two shallow drawers under it and, yes, a pile of brightly-coloured pamphlets beside it—was plainly empty. Its door had crashed right back against the wall. There was nowhere where anybody could be crouched ready to spring.

The moment he had realized this he had jumped back into the big, bare main room and had braced himself to meet an onslaught from someone coming hurtling out through the other door with that terribly honed knife raised high. After the explosion of noise the door he had thrust open had made he could expect nothing else.

One second passed. Two. Three.

They were taking their time. Perhaps they had succeeded in checking their immediate impulse to come rushing out. Perhaps they had decided they would do better to wait for the intruder to come to them.

And perhaps they were right. They would know exactly what to expect now. The swift turning of the door-knob, followed immediately by the door banging hard back. So they could plan their counter-action in advance. Be ready, tensed to spring, from whatever part of the little bathroom best suited their purpose.

So should he too wait it out?

He was tempted. It would be a lot less frightening than going head first into danger. But a moment's thought made him realize that the killer in the bathroom would not wait for ever. If they were to stay in there too long they would be trapped. The ashram disciples would begin to stir perhaps as early as five o'clock so as to be ready for the announcement that Swami was supposed to be going to make at six. There was always the chance, too, that someone would be about even earlier. It would need only a shout to summon them. And once there was more than one person to deal with the chance of escape would be cut away to almost nothing. No, they could not afford to wait too long.

So at some time in the next few minutes that door would fly open and he would be confronted with a murderer armed with a deadly knife. Better then to attack first again himself.

And, if that was to be done, do it at once.

He drew in one long deep breath, tensed himself, darted forward, jerked round the handle of the bathroom door, stepped back and with his right foot gave the door a thudding full-soled kick.

It swung wide. The light from the big room behind him flooded in.

He jumped back, crouched and waited for the onrush.

One long second. Another.

'Freeze, fella. Get 'em up.'

The shouted words had come not from the bathroom in front of him but from behind. He obeyed the command, even though he had only half understood it. He raised both his hands clear into the air above his head.

Then he slowly turned round.

A huge burly man in a blue uniform had burst into the room and was standing, legs well apart, knees slightly bent, holding in two big bony hands a short-barrelled, pump-action shotgun.

'Okay, dude,' he said. 'You coming quietly, or am I going to have to shoot your legs off?'

CHAPTER SEVEN

For a moment Inspector Ghote thought he was going to find himself arrested by a fellow officer on a charge of murdering the man he had come to California to challenge. Then common sense reasserted itself.

'Good evening,' he said. 'I am most glad you have arrived upon the scene. I myself had only just entered this room and found this body in the condition in which you see it. I very much welcome your arrival.'

But even as he said the words it occurred to him that in fact the arrival of the California police at this exact moment was altogether extraordinary. The Swami had been killed little more than ten minutes before. No one else but himself knew. So how was it that the police were here already?

And hard on the heels of that thought came another.

Where was the Swami's murderer? In the few instants between the time he himself had flung back the door of the bathroom and the moment he had turned to face this big man with the shotgun he had seen right into the little cubicle. And it had been as bare as the bedroom beside it. There was a shower with its glass door pushed right back. There was a wash-basin.

There was a lavatory-bowl, western-style. And nothing else. There was nowhere that anyone, however small, however crouched, could possibly have hidden.

So where was the person who had killed Swami? And where was the knife they had used?

'You trying something?' the man at the door asked, heavy with suspicion.

'No, no. Please allow me to explain. I have only just come into this building. When I opened the door where you are now standing I saw there on the floor the body of the man they are calling the Swami With No Name. I saw too that he had only just been killed. His blood was still liquid, you know. And I thought that whoever had done the deed was very, very likely to be concealed in one of these two little rooms here because I had seen no one come out, you know. I was carrying out an investigation when you entered.'

'You sure are trying something.'

The cop—Ghote thought suddenly that this was what he ought to be calling the fellow—shouted out to someone in the lobby behind him, his shotgun not wavering by as much as a whisker.

'Hey, come on in here. We got some sorta kook.'

In at the door came a second cop, as big, as raw-boned, as fresh-faced.

Ghote decided that he must dispel as quickly

111

as possible the idea that he was a kook. Whatever exactly a kook was.

'Gentlemen,' he said, with all the confidence he could muster, 'perhaps I had better introduce myself. I am Inspector Ghote of the Bombay police. I am here making private inquiries on behalf of a very, very influential Bombay citizen. In the course of those inquiries I had occasion to enter this room some few minutes ago only and here, as I have stated, I discovered the body of the Swami With No Name.'

'Well, we saw him go in so he ain't fooling about that,' the second of the two cops said, though he sounded distinctly doubtful.

'Yeah, I guess. But . . .'

The cop with the shotgun, still held rock-steady, was more dubious.

'Inspector?' said his companion. 'You got any ID?'

'Idee? That is idea?' Ghote asked eagerly. 'But I must tell you, gentlemen, I have not got any idea at all. You see, it is altogether most strange. I am coming in here, as I have told. I am seeing the body, with the throat cut and the blood flowing still. I saw that with my own eyes. So he cannot have been dead for more than a few minutes, not more than ten at most. That you must be knowing. But, gentlemen, where is the weapon that cut his throat? I am able—'

'ID he said, fella,' the cop with the gun growled. 'ID. You know what ID is?'

112

'No,' Ghote said.

The shotgun did turn away a little now. The cop holding it was evidently so exasperated by this appalling ignorance that he had to look at his companion to see his reaction.

'The guy ain't no Inspector, that's for sure,' he said. 'If you ask me, he's some sorta wetback, come straight over the Mex border.'

'Nah, he ain't no Mexican.'

Ghote broke in before the argument could go any further.

'Gentlemen, I can assure you I am exactly as stated. Please, will you allow me to put down my hands and take from my wallet my card?'

'ID,' said the cop with the gun. 'Now you got ID.'

'Okay, fella, go ahead,' said his companion. 'But watch it.'

Ghote, making an effort to show himself completely calm, lowered his hands, took his wallet from his inner pocket, extracted one of his cards—how strange the familiar pasteboard he so often had occasion to hand to people back at home looked now—and held it out at arm's length in front of him.

The second cop, taking good care not to go between Ghote and his companion with the shotgun, came over, plucked the card from his outstretched fingers and read it aloud.

'Inspector G. V. Goat, Detection of Crime Branch, Bombay.'

113

The shotgun at last was lowered.

'We'd better get some brass out here fast,' the cop with it said. 'This is just crazy.'

The other cop went over to the white telephone, hunkered down beside it and punched out a number on its buttons.

'Put me on to the Lieutenant,' he said after a few moments. 'Lieutenant? Deputy Barnes here, sir. At that place, the ashram. We have a DB, sir. Yes, sir. With his throat cut and—And, well, sir, no weapon visible and—And, I guess, no way for any killer to have gotten away, sir. So will you—Yes, sir. Be glad to see you, sir. And, sir, one other thing. Well, sir, we have a witness here, practically an eyeball wit to the killing, sir, but—But, sir, it seems he's a cop, a cop from Bombay, India. And, sir, he's real top brass. An Inspector, no less. So, if you'd—Yes, sir. Right away, Lieutenant, sir.'

He put down the receiver and stood up with a little grunt of effort.

'Says to say Welcome aboard, Inspector, sir,' he said.

Ghote, who had worked out during the latter part of the call that police ranks in America must differ from those in India and that he had thus been placed a good deal higher up the tree than was his right, decided to say nothing for the time being. The two cops had quite enough to take in already.

Instead he suggested that they ought to verify

114

his own findings before any more time had passed. He very much wanted them to do so. What he had discovered seemed impossible to believe.

He went over to Swami's yellow silk-covered cushion throne while they began their exploration, feeling abruptly exhausted by all that had happened in the last few minutes. For a moment, just as he was about to sink down on to the mattress, a sudden absurdly fanciful idea assailed him. What if he was to flop down right on to the killer concealed somehow among the cushions?

But even before he had lifted the mattress and given each yellow-covered cushion a savage prod he knew that really it would have been out of the question for anyone to have rearranged the throne so neatly within the very short time between the moment the Swami's throat must have been cut and his own entry.

So where was the killer? And where was the weapon they had used? Even that was not hidden anywhere in the throne. His probing had made sure of that.

He sank down on to the mattress and put his head between his two hands, only looking up when after a considerable interval the two cops emerged, one from the bedroom, the other from the bathroom. As they did so they paused and looked at each other. Their wide shoulders rose in two huge shrugs.

'Well, Inspector, sir,' said the one who had named himself on the telephone as Deputy Barnes, 'I guess you're one hundred per cent right. There's no one in this whole crazy building. There's no way either that anyone could have gotten out. And there's no weapon in here. I guess it's . . . Well, I guess I'm glad the lieutenant's on his way.'

After this the three of them waited in an embarrassed silence. Each from time to time cast a surreptitious glance round the big square room as if trying to imagine somewhere in its bareness where a man, or even a woman, could still somehow be hidden.

Or where something as small as a knife, a knife with a razor-thin cutting edge, might be concealed.

But none of them, as the minutes crawled by, hit on even enough of a wild supposition to make it worth suggesting aloud.

At last there came the distant sound of a car climbing the track up the hill in low gear.

'Guess I'd better show,' said the cop with the shotgun.

He stomped over to the door and went out, relief at being able to depart plain on his wind-tanned ruddy face.

Deputy Barnes gave Ghote a half-rueful look.

'Lieutenant Foster'll be here in a coupla minutes, I guess,' he said.

'Yes,' Ghote answered.

116

Then abruptly a question he had meant to ask earlier came back to him.

'But please,' he said, 'how was it that the two of you came upon the scene with such rapidity? I have not at all understood that.'

'Yeah,' said Deputy Barnes. 'Well, I guess if you're an Inspector it'll be okay to tell you.'

'Oh, yes,' Ghote said, drawing himself up a little on the Swami's yellow throne. 'Quite all right, quite all right.'

'Well, it's like this, Inspector. This—this Swami guy, he was due to be interviewed by the lieutenant tonight. Lieutenant had wanted to see him this evening, but the guy said he had some sorta prayer meeting he had to hold. Something that'd go on till past midnight. I dunno how they do that sorta thing out here. So could the lieutenant come out late tonight? Well, I guess the lieutenant wanted to play it cool. It was religion an' all, and the Swami guy had a lotta friends too, you know.'

'Yes, yes. It is the same in Bombay, I assure you.'

'That so? Yeah. Well. Well, all the same the lieutenant didn't wanna risk the guy high-tailing it. So he sends the two of us out here. Park the unit outa sight down the bottom of the hill, come up on foot and surveillance the place.'

'And you saw nothing? No one coming out of here?'

'All we saw was you, Inspector. You kinda

117

creeping up on this cabin. And, well, sir, I guess we didn't know . . .'

'Yes, yes. You did quite right. A person behaving in a suspicious manner. You did quite right.'

'Thank you, sir. Here's the lieutenant now, I guess.'

The sound of an exchange of conversation in low voices had been audible. Ghote got to his feet and waited for the newcomer.

The man who came in with the burly, shotgun toting cop was a little shorter than the majority of tall Americans Ghote had so far seen. He was dressed in a quiet grey lightweight suit with a plain white shirt. He wore a tie, a dark blue one with a thin white stripe in it. But what chiefly struck Ghote was his eyes. They were grey and cold-looking in his tanned face. And from the moment he had come in they had been making assessments, calmly moving from the Swami's dead body with its cascade of curling black locks and gaping throat to the cushion-piled yellow throne, from Deputy Barnes to him himself.

And all this in the few instants between his stepping through the doorway and his walking over with hand out-thrust.

'Lieutenant Foster, Inspector. Pleased to meet you. I guess rank-wise you and I are pretty well on a par in our respective forces.'

'Yes,' Ghote answered, at once glad he no

118

longer had to pretend to be more important than he was. 'And I am most glad also to meet you, Lieutenant.'

He had pronounced lieutenant in the American way and not in the British nor in its simplified Hindi equivalent. He felt that by doing so he had really put himself on equal terms.

'So I'd be glad to know just what you're doing here,' Lieutenant Foster said.

Bleakly.

Ghote swallowed.

'I am here in a private capacity only,' he answered, unable now to add a lieutenant. 'I am acting on behalf of Mr Ranjee Shahani, a very, very influential Bombay businessman. It is at the request of our State Minister for Police Affairs. Mr Shahani's daughter has become what we are calling a *chela* at the ashram here, and her father believes she is being detained against her will. I am investigating the matter.'

'On your own?' Lieutenant Foster asked, his grey eyes homing in once again.

Ghote hesitated.

Should he mention that Fred Hoskins had also been retained by Mr Shahani, at Rupees 2,000 a day plus expenses? Or ought he to conceal that confidential fact? If he mentioned the private eye—and was this the real reason for his reluctance to do so?—would not Fred Hoskins, as soon as he had been contacted, convey to the lieutenant his own low opinion of him himself? Of a man, a cop, who failed to carry a piece? Who was so short in stature? Who was unfit to meet his ex-colleagues of the LAPD? And he very much wanted, he found suddenly, to gain the good opinion of this quiet, watchful man.

He decided to gloss over Fred Hoskins's part in his inquiry. But then something in those grey, reasoning eyes looking at him so intently made him abruptly change his mind.

'There is an American detective also,' he said. 'What you are calling a private eye. Known by the name of Fred Hoskins.'

'Thank you,' said Lieutenant Foster.

He turned to the cop who had come in with him.

'Better call Hoskins in,' he said laconically.

A sweat-hot wave of relief swamped Ghote. How appallingly he would have been discredited in the eyes of this cool, quiet man if he had glossed over Fred Hoskins's existence. How utterly he would have lost his status of being on a par with the Californian officer.

Fred Hoskins came in at the door.

'So, Gan boy,' he said loudly, 'I met up with Lieutenant Foster here and I hear you've got yourself a Murder One.'

But Lieutenant Foster gave Ghote no time to answer, no time even to ask just what a Murder One was.

'Inspector,' he said, his low, level voice in strong contrast to Fred Hoskins's twanging yammer. 'What you tell me about Miss Shahani is of considerable interest to me. I won't make any bones about it. Los Angeles County Sheriff's Department has received complaints about this place, complaints similar in outline to the one you're investigating. I was due to interview the Swami tonight. At 1 a.m. when he said he'd be through with a meditation session he had to hold. It looks as if maybe someone's taken the law into their own hands and anticipated me.'

'Yes. Yes, a murder for some reason of that sort,' Ghote said. 'I see that. But . . .'

'But what, Inspector?'

'But how can it be, Lieutenant? When I first saw the Swami's body his blood was still liquid, still flowing from the wound. And yet I had had under my personal observation for at least ten minutes beforehand the only means of exit from this building.'

'That so? It's what I gathered from the deputy here, but I figured there'd been some misunderstanding.'

The lieutenant's serious tanned face betrayed a fleeting look of puzzlement, and Ghote guessed that it was rare for the man to allow any feelings or thoughts he might have to show themselves as openly.

'Lieutenant.'

121

Fred Hoskins's voice splattered into the quiet of the bare room.

Lieutenant Foster flicked his grey eyes in his direction.

'Lieutenant, if my understanding of this situation is correct and you're faced with a corpse with no murderer and no weapon in sight, then I can tell you you're a very lucky man.'

'Hoskins, I'll talk to you in good time,' Lieutenant Foster answered.

He turned back to Ghote.

'So, Inspector, I'd appreciate it if you would give me any co-operation I may request. It appears—'

'But that's just what you don't see, Lieutenant,' came the hammer-hammer-hammer voice from behind them. 'It's just the co-operation of this distinguished visitor that makes you so lucky. He's an Indian, Lieutenant. An Indian Indian. A Hindu. He's the very person you're looking for.'

'I'm looking for the person who did that, Hoskins.'

The lieutenant's cold eyes indicated the Swami's sprawled body on the bare clean boards of the floor.

'I'm looking for the killer here, and I don't think Inspector Ghote fits the bill.'

'You're under a false impression, if I may say so, Lieutenant,' Fred Hoskins battered on, unabashed. 'The reason you're in a position of great strength is that it's obvious that this is no ordinary crime. It's no more than a perfect example of crime committed by means of oriental magic, and right here beside you, Lieutenant, you have a top expert in oriental magic.'

'No!'

Ghote, outraged, exploded with the word before perhaps better counsel could prevail.

And at once he found himself looking straight into those cold, appraising eyes.

He felt obliged to offer an explanation.

'Lieutenant,' he said, 'I would not disguise from you that in my country, and perhaps it is so also in other parts of the world, events do occur which can be called magic, events which cannot be accounted for by logical, scientific means. I was thinking not very long ago of such an incident within my own experience. In Lamington Road Gaol, Bombay, we had occasion to put behind bars a fellow we suspected of an offence against Indian Penal Code Section 508, inducing a person to believe he will become the object of divine displeasure. In fact, the fellow we had nabbed was not the man who had committed that particular offence. However, there he was behind bars. There at night the officer in charge left him. There also on one occasion I myself saw him. But, Lieutenant, on each and every morning of that

123

period when routine inspection was carried out the man was found to be sitting quietly on the outer side of those bars. This is a thing that happened. I do not know how it can be accounted for, but it took place.'

He saw no look of belief enter the grey eyes that had held him throughout his narrative. But he had hardly expected to do so.

He added then the sentence he had intended to add from the beginning.

'Such things happen, Lieutenant, but nevertheless I see no reason why such an explanation should be resorted to in the present circumstances.'

'All right, Inspector,' said the lieutenant. 'What you've told me about the guy in your gaol is contrary to anything I'm ever going to believe. I'll tell you that. But I also accept that, for good reasons of your own, you do give credence to such—'

He paused an instant.

'To such accounts. However, I'm interested in your reasoning here.'

'For such events to take place,' Ghote said, 'there must be an individual present with the powers that are required. In the length and breadth of India there are, I am certain, a number of such individuals alive today and there have also been many of them in past ages.'

'Yeah, but the Swami here,' Fred Hoskins broke jarringly in. 'There was a guy with mystic

124

powers.'

'No, you are wrong,' Ghote said, without hesitation. 'You are entirely wrong, Mr Hoskins. Yes, the Swami possessed certain unusual powers. He was able earlier today to realize that I, a complete stranger who had only just entered the hall where he was, that I was suffering from a severe headache even though he was many yards distant from me. And he was able also to cure that headache with one touch of his hand. But he did not possess powers in any way greater than that.'

'And why was this?' Lieutenant Foster asked quietly.

'Because the fellow was a cheat only,' Ghote answered. 'A proven cheat.'

CHAPTER EIGHT

Ghote hoped for a word of approval from Lieutenant Foster for that confident assertion of his, based on the one swift glimpse he had had of the car brochures, that the Swami With No Name, whatever healing power he might possess, was no mysterious wonder-worker but a familiar confidence trickster. But, though he thought he had seen a hint of quick pleasure in those cool grey eyes, the lieutenant was given no opportunity to speak. From Fred Hoskins, at

125

the door of the big bare room, there came a roar of anguished rage that obliterated everything.

'No,' he yelled. 'No. Jeez, there's nothing pisses me off more than to hear a guy try and talk himself out of an assignment that fits him like a goddam glove. Don't listen to him, Lieutenant. You got yourself the only guy who can solve this case. You can't tell me this isn't some kind of magic happening here, and right in front of you you've got the one guy who knows about Hindu magic from A to Z.'

But the lieutenant remained unimpressed.

When Fred Hoskins had finished he simply turned to Deputy Barnes and began giving him orders to get hold of someone in authority at the ashram. Ghote got only a terse inquiry as to whether he knew where Nirmala Shahani now was, and when he said that he at least knew the name of the hut where she slept, Shanti Sadan, he was asked to get hold of her if he could.

So, instead of rapidly solving the case under the patronage of Fred Hoskins, he found himself after he had brought Nirmala to the lieutenant left standing with nothing to do. He leant against a tree just outside the central circle of ashram buildings, with behind him the night made noisy by the arrival of vehicle after vehicle bringing in the technicians of the Sheriff's Department murder investigation team.

In front of him there stretched the dark mass of night-hidden redwoods. Above were the stars

126

in a cloudless sky.

But the scene was not peaceful. At his elbow Fred Hoskins was talking.

For little reason that Ghote could see, at first, the hulking private-eye was giving him a detailed top-to-bottom guide to the Los Angeles Police Department. Figures of frightening size poured out. Statistics tumbled forth. Until at last there emerged the fact that there had once been in the force a certain Fred Hoskins who, because of various hinted-at jealousies and pieces of appalling ill-luck, had never risen beyond the lowliest of grades, patrolman.

'So I retired, Gan boy. But how do you think I retired? I'm asking you that.'

Ghote had been listening only because listening was better than putting to himself uselessly time and again the question how it could be that the Swami had met his death in a place where there was no weapon and no way a weapon could have been taken out. He realized abruptly now that the hammering stream of sound had come to a temporary halt with a query he was supposed to find an answer for.

'How did you retire? I am not having any idea whatsoever. Fred.'

It appeared that that response would do. Fred Hoskins cheerfully thumped a vast palm with a vast fist.

'Then I'll tell you, Gan boy. I did not retire as a hasbeen. No, sir. I retired as an am-right-now.

I quit at age forty-two with a pension of one thousand dollars per month, and the very next day I opened an office as a PI in downtown LA. And, let me tell you, Gan, I haven't looked back since.'

'That is very good.'

But Fred Hoskins paid no attention to this modest, and hypocritical, morsel of praise.

'Now,' he said, 'I'm gonna put you in the picture about the LAPD's brother force, the Sheriff's Department, among whose personnel I number some very good friends, not excluding Lieutenant Foster.'

'Thank you. Fred.'

Thanks, however, were not needed. Another torrent of factual information had been embarked upon. Words banged ceaselessly once more into the pine-scented night air.

'A total of sworn personnel in excess of five thousand . . . a computerized gas chromatograph . . . as many as nine hundred radio-equipped mobile units . . . in excess of fifteen 'copters . . . snowmobiles . . . dune buggies . . .'

What on earth is a dune buggy, Ghote wondered. And all that other transport. Into his mind, so clearly that he almost felt it to be present, there came an image of one of the cars of the Bombay police in which he had so often gone out on an investigation, of its scuffed grey leather seats, its crackling radio over which it

128

was hard to make out even the simplest of messages, of the number crudely painted in white on the dashboard in accordance with regulations.

But no amount of comparing Californian opulence with Bombay make-do could for long push out of his head the mental search he kept conducting and re-conducting of the big bare room in which the Swami With No Name had met his death. The close-fitting boards of its floor, the yellow cushion-throne, the blank doors of bedroom and bathroom, the blank windowless walls.

Well, perhaps all the technical equipment at the command of the Sheriff's Department— through the open double doors of the Swami's house there had been coming the regular intense blue flashes of photographs being taken— perhaps these would provide the answer that he could not even imagine. The simple, logical answer.

And Fred Hoskins was yammering on.

'. . . flexible communications computer maintains a book-keeping function and also equally distributes incoming traffic among the many radio-dispatching positions. This computer is capable of sensing an incoming digital message and of assigning the same to an electronic console within fifty milliseconds at the same time that it provides the console with all the transmitters, receivers, telephone lines and status signals necessary for . . .'

Do we have status signals at Crawford Market headquarters, he asked himself. And anyhow what is a status signal?

He very much doubted whether such things played any part in the operation of the ingenious file-flapping mechanical device that was the pride of Records Section at the Detection of Crime Branch. But they did not do so badly, he reflected, when it came to putting criminals behind the bars.

'I would like to conclude this topic,' the voice beside him twanged on, 'by listing some of the . . .'

But in the darkness of the central circle of buildings a sudden swathe of bright light cut out from the administration block. In it, as he turned, Ghote saw the small, sari-clad figure of Nirmala Shahani. Lieutenant Foster had finished interviewing her.

He strode off in her direction, leaving the huge private eye still listing whatever it was he had been determined to list. Nirmala Shahani was his duty. He was not here, he told himself sharply, to rack his brains pointlessly in trying to think how the Swami could have been killed. He was here in California simply on behalf of Mr Ranjee Shahani, of Shahani Enterprises Private Ltd, to see that his daughter was returned safely to Bombay, to her already arranged marriage there with the financial benefits that would bring, to the world of comfort and order.

'Kumari Shahani,' he called out.

At the sound of the Hindi words the girl stopped and stood peering into the darkness.

Ghote came quickly up.

'Good morning again, Miss Shahani,' he said. 'Now is there anything I can do to assist you?'

The girl looked at him in silence. In the dark he had largely to imagine that soft face of hers with its yet softer, new-born animal nose.

'I do not think I would get any assistance from the man who tried to make me turn my back on Swamiji,' she said.

'But—'

Surely the stupid creature could not still be believing that the Swami was the godlike person she had once thought him to be. But perhaps she did not yet know that close beside the man's bed there lay that pile of brightly coloured car brochures. A pity that with Lieutenant Foster's technicians still swarming all over the house he could not march her in there at this very moment and make her see how wrong she had been. Well, she would just have to take his word for it.

'Miss Shahani, I think you do not understand. Perhaps Lieutenant Foster did not tell you everything. You know that I was the person who discovered Swami's body? I went into his house when he was meant to be in the

131

Meditation Hall in a state of *samadhi* and while I was there I saw beside Swami's bed a large pile of brochures for motor-cars.'

'Cars.' The girl spat the word out. 'What are cars mattering now? How can we know why Swamiji had those brochures there? They mean nothing now.'

'Well, that is not exactly so, you know. They still do mean that Swami was very, very interested in selecting the best and most expensive gift for Mrs Russell Walters to give him. I know that it must hurt you to hear this. But it is the fact. Swami lied to Mrs Russell Walters when he was saying he did not know anything about cars, and he lied also in saying that he was going to spend the whole of this night in meditation. Swami was no more than a common cheat only. Miss Shahani, let me take you now back to Los Angeles where we would find you a hotel. And tomorrow we will take the first available flight to Bombay.'

'You fool.'

The words rang out like bell-strokes in the clear, cool night.

Ghote took half a step backwards. He could still just see that pretty, soft-nosed face. It was glaring at him.

'Do you think I did not know that Swamiji did not intend to stay in the Meditation Hall?' Nirmala demanded. 'He had told me that he would want to see me during the night. In his

132

own house. He said I would know when to come. He would put the thought into my head. But in the end he never had time to do that.'

At least that last claim was probably true, Ghote thought. The girl had been fast asleep when he had found the hut called Shanti Sadan. But, never mind about whether Swami had or had not said he would remain in the Meditation Hall, there was still the matter of the motor-car brochures. The fellow was a liar. And he was greedy.

'Very well,' he said stiffly. 'There is still the question of his lies about cars. It is no use to say it does not matter. Those brochures were in his room. I saw them. They are there. They prove he was not at all a truth-telling person. Miss Shahani, come with me now. Mr Hoskins will drive us to Los Angeles.'

'How can you be so stupid?'

He saw the girl stamp petulantly on the pine-needle soft ground. And a corresponding rage swept up in him.

'I am stupid?' he said. 'Let me tell you, it is you who are being stupid, stupid. Please think about what I have told. Swami lied. He lied and he showed himself also to be as greedy for possessions as any of the people in the West he was denouncing. That is the truth, Miss. Kindly accept it.'

'Won't you see?' the girl stormed back at him. 'Won't you see what is in front of your eyes?

133

Swamiji had troubles, many, many troubles. More than you could know. The time had come for him to go. To go from this terrible, materialistic country. To go altogether from the world. But when he went he left behind him a sign. A sign that told, for ever and for ever, that he was a great soul, that he could do those things that only the greatest souls can do.'

Thoughts tumbled and cascaded in Ghote's mind like the shards in a violently shaken kaleidoscope. Tumbled and cascaded, and fell into a new unexpected pattern.

'You mean— You mean that Swami committed suicide?' he said. 'Cut his own throat and then caused the knife he had done it with to disappear?'

'Of course.'

It was possible. Provided you were willing to accept that Swami possessed the powers Nirmala believed he had. There was nothing in logic to say that he had not taken his own life rather than been murdered. If the weapon had disappeared by means unknown to science, then suicide was just as likely as murder. And suicide was a clear possibility if the man had had mysterious troubles about which he himself knew nothing. Or very little. Because, after all, Lieutenant Foster had been going to come to the ashram originally to investigate, not Swami's death, but his activities while he had been alive. Activities that might have included summoning

134

pretty, innocent, defenceless Nirmala to his house in the middle of the night.

He was about to admit, cautiously, that what she had said might be part of the truth when she spoke again.

'Now do you see at last? Swamiji was a great soul, a true yogi. He has put thousands in the East as well as in the West on to the path. It was the most wonderful thing that ever happened to me that one day in Los Angeles I went to hear him talk just because I was homesick and he came from India. I thought I wanted to hear an Indian voice only, and I found that my whole life had been altered.'

'Yes, I see that,' Ghote conceded reluctantly.

It was still plain to him, despite what Nirmala had said, that the Swami was at best very dubious. And it was still his duty to get the girl away from this place and back to Bombay. Everyday Bombay.

'I am sure,' he went on, picking his way word by word, 'that you will remember Swamiji as long as you live. He will be a great, great influence on you. Even you will tell your children about him and they will—'

'What children?' Nirmala interrupted sharply.

'Well, I am sure that you will one day get married. Perhaps that will be sooner than you think even. Once you are back in Bombay you would—'

135

'I am not going back to Bombay. I am not leaving the ashram. I am staying here all my life, devoting myself to Swamiji's memory, meditating in the way that he taught us.'

'But— But— But surely the ashram will pack up now. The whole place was Swami's idea, isn't it? And now that he— Now that he has gone, it will have to come to an end. You are distressed, Miss Shahani. Let me take you to a hotel.'

'Won't you ever understand? Have you seen nothing here? Do you think Swamiji had no influence on anybody? There are hundreds of people who will stay here and come here. I will be only one of them.'

'Well, yes, I expect there will be others who feel as you do. But all the same I think that you will find that quite soon... You see, you will all be without any leader whatsoever, and that is not an easy situation to overcome... You know, I still think it would be best for you to go home, for a little while at least. Then you can see—'

'You idiot. You *bewakoof*. Haven't you seen Johnananda? Couldn't you tell that he would be the ashram's leader? Swami made him his deputy. Now he takes the mantle.'

'But— But he is an Englishman.'

'Does God made any difference between Indian and Englishman? Between Indian and American? Swamiji bequeathed his mission to

136

Johnananda. It will be Johnananda who sees that Swamiji's book is published, that it goes all over the world. Millions and millions are going to find the way because of it. Swamiji said so. That is what Johnananda will do. And I will be one of those that help him. Here. In the ashram. Which will become a world-renowned shrine. Here. Here. Here.'

Ghote stood, suddenly chilled in the diamond-starred Californian night, and wished with all his might that at this very instant someone would come bursting out of Swami's house shouting into the cool quietness 'I got it, I got it, I found the weapon.'

But there was no sound other than muffled voices from anywhere within the circle of ashram buildings and the stars twinkled emptily as ever.

'Miss Shahani,' he said wearily, 'believe me, I am very well understanding your feelings at this moment. You have spent weeks as a devoted disciple of that man. He had captured you entirely. But, please, I have proved to you that he was a liar and an altogether greedy individual. Please try to take that in. Miss Shahani, there will not be a shrine here. Swami was not the man to cause a shrine to grow up. He was not. In a few months only this place will be deserted altogether.'

'When all the world has heard how Swamiji took his own life and made the knife that he used disappear? Made it disappear so that no one, however much scientific apparatus they are using, will ever find it? Do you believe that?'

And Ghote had to admit to himself that, if what she had described did come about, it was possible, more than possible even, that a cult would spring up here. And that man had been a cheat. A cheat. A figure on a footing with the idle, cash-seeking bhaghat he himself had detected playing the mango-tree trick at the Azad Maidan.

'If that knife did not disappear by means of extra-ordinary powers,' he said, feeling each word sound like a hollow drumbeat within himself. 'If Swami made it disappear by some trick only, what then, Miss Shahani? Would you come with me back to Bombay then?'

'You want to clean the sky with a broom?' Nirmala said scornfully.

'If Swami did take his own life, then he has hidden the weapon by common cheating,' Ghote answered. 'I swear that to you, and I will prove it to you.'

He had known he was going to make that promise, a promise a hundred times harder to keep than his pledge to show that Swami had lied over the car brochures. But as he heard the words come out of his mouth he felt a plunging sense of appalled dismay. What had he undertaken to do?

CHAPTER NINE

It took Inspector Ghote a long time before he was able to put to Lieutenant Foster the request to have a full share in his investigation of the Swami's death that he felt he must make. He had seen how inescapable that would be within minutes of his pledge to Nirmala Shahani. Without the lieutenant's co-operation he would never get anywhere.

So he had stationed himself where in the darkness of the starlit night he had a good view of the entrance to the ashram's administration block and he had watched patiently for a moment when the lieutenant should be free.

In any gap in the series of interviews the lieutenant was conducting, or if he should happen to step outside for a breath of air, he felt he could go over to him and put his request. But what he was certain he should not do was to crash in on him without ceremony. The chances of meeting with a rebuff were in any case so great—he himself, if this investigation were taking place in Bombay, would send off any visiting American wanting to poke his nose in pretty damn quick—that the least he could do was to judge the moment to put himself forward with the maximum care.

Besides, he did not deep down want to make

the request at all. It would mean pretending to the lieutenant that after all he did believe that there was an element of the supernatural in the case. Because the only way his request would stand a chance, he had decided, was if he said that he had now changed his mind about the way in which the weapon has disappeared. He was going to have to put himself forward as Fred Hoskins's expert—heaven help him—in Hindu magic.

Certainly, were he to go round putting questions to people purely on his own account, word would soon get back to the lieutenant, and then he would very likely find himself charge-sheeted. Under whatever was the Californian equivalent of Indian Penal Code Section 186, obstructing a public servant in the discharge of his public functions.

No, there was only one way of proving to that little fool Nirmala Shahani—that little fool he would have liked to have been his own daughter—that the Swami she so much venerated was a common fake. And that was to convince that cool, grey-eyed man in the administration block at this moment that there was a real possibility that powers beyond the ordinary had played a part in the Swami's death.

But perhaps, even yet, one of the computers at the lieutenant's command would whirr and whirl and somehow produce an entirely logical hiding-place for the missing murder weapon to be. Perhaps it was just a matter of using the right status signals.

Time went slowly by.

But there was no sign in the single brightly-lit window of the administration block that Lieutenant Foster was ever disengaged. From time to time Ghote heard him call an order to the deputy who stood on the block's wooden entrance steps. 'Tell that Johnananda guy I'd like another word, please' or 'Go across and see if there's any progress over there, goddammit.' But orders to fetch anyone always came when someone else was already shut in the office with the lieutenant, and the deputy, who went across to the Swami's house at the double, always came back again within minutes.

It began to grow distinctly cold.

Ghote held his watch up to catch the distant light from Lieutenant Foster's window to see what time it was and guess whether sunrise was near. But the damn thing still seemed to be registering the time for somewhere between Bombay and Los Angeles, wherever it had been that he had last remembered to adjust it.

Then, through the tall redwoods at last, he caught a glimpse of a faint line of white on the horizon. Dawn. The start of a new day. What would it bring? How could it produce a solution to that absurd problem of the throat cut without any trace of the weapon that had cut it?

Time and again he had felt his mind bang

141

hard up against that unyielding blank, as if it was, he thought, a sodden article of washing being battered and battered by a dhobi on to a flat unbreakable area of stone. How can a man be killed and the instrument that killed him disappear from a windowless room of which the sole exit had been under constant observation?

He shook himself.

Before long all the ashram disciples would be up and about. Their presence was certain to affect the lieutenant. Either he would come out to them, perhaps to tell them all assembled what had happened and what he and his men were doing about it, or, more likely, he would decide to move the centre of operations out of the ashram to somewhere where his every move would not be watched. So the moment for making that difficult request could not be far off.

The moment when he would have to go back on the firm assertion he had made that the crime was, whatever appearances might indicate, a simple matter of logic. The moment when he would have to admit—an admission all the more bitter for being, ironically, untrue—that perhaps after all he did believe that mysterious powers had been at work.

'Gan, boy, there you are. Where the hell did you get to? I've been looking all over for you. I wanted to tell you your great opportunity is here.'

142

Ghote, who had hoped that at some time since he had left Fred Hoskins's side to go and talk to Nirmala the belly-swaggering private-eye had taken himself off to bed, turned with a sigh to confront that looming figure once more.

'Good morning, Fred,' he offered.

'Yes, sir. The good lieutenant will soon be emerging. When he does, unless I am very much mistaken he'll have finally come to the conclusion that this is a matter involving Hindu magical powers. He will now be ready to ask for your co-operation, and I'll be happy to take the opportunity to inform him of that fact.'

Inspector Ghote found he was standing, with unexpected suddenness, on the edge of a deep pool of troubled boiling bubbling mud. Stood for an instant. Plunged.

'Fred, I would be very happy for you to tell the lieutenant that I will use my knowledge of Hindu mystical powers to assist him in any way I can.'

He saw, with faint far-off pleasure, Fred Hoskins jolt back with surprise.

And at that very moment a broad bar of light streamed out from the administration block doorway into the scarcely dawn-touched darkness. In it, yawning and stretching with cat-neat movements, stood Lieutenant Foster.

'Lieutenant, Lieutenant,' Fred Hoskins promptly hollered. 'I've got great news for you. Great news.'

143

He went striding across to where the lieutenant stood, suddenly alert. Ghote followed him, wishing hard he was going in exactly the opposite direction.

'Lieutenant, I have just pressured my very good friend, Inspector Goat, top expert in Hindu magical practices, into volunteering his assistance to you.'

The lieutenant did not snap out the curt dismissal Ghote had expected, and secretly half-hoped for even though it would reduce almost to nothing his chances of proving to Nirmala Shahani that the Swami's death involved no miracle. Instead he stood on the lowest step of the administration block entrance looking impenetrably into the middle distance.

Then he turned to Ghote.

'Inspector,' he said, 'you might as well know, just what's been produced by one hell of a lot of hard work ever since we arrived here. Zilch. Precisely zilch. We have no explanation whatever of where the murder weapon is. My men have gone over every inch of the walls there, every inch of that floor. They're solid. They've ripped the plumbing apart. They've dismantled the telephone. They've checked that statue out in the lobby to prove it's solid too, just like the pillar it stands on. There's no way a knife could have been taken or thrown out of there. And you weren't the only one to have those doors under observation. My two deputies

144

had them in full sight for longer than you did. They confirm the fact that exactly no one and nothing came out of them.'

He came to a halt. A yet bleaker expression appeared on his face.

'Inspector,' he said, 'if you're willing to hang around, well, I guess I'm not going to offer any objections.'

Ghote felt for him. The very obliqueness of his appeal made it all the clearer how hard it must have been for him to make it. To admit that here in California, in America, there might have been committed a crime that could not be solved except by admitting that supernatural powers existed.

'Lieutenant,' he said, 'it seems that Miss Shahani is not yet quite ready to return to Bombay, so I shall be staying here a little longer. If during that time I may be permitted to observe the procedures of the Los Angeles County Sheriff's Department I would be very, very grateful.'

'Be glad to show you around,' Lieutenant Foster answered, his tones clipped to curtness. 'Very glad.'

'But, hell, Lieutenant,' Fred Hoskins burst in, 'you oughta take full advantage of—'

'Mr Hoskins,' Ghote said sharply, 'I expect Lieutenant Foster will allow you also to come with us. But we must not in any way hinder his work.'

145

Somewhat to his surprise the towering private eye fell into a dead silence.

'Lieutenant,' Ghote said, 'when you told that you had learnt—was it?—zilch in all you have done, was there nothing at all that you discovered?'

The lieutenant sighed.

'Oh, hell, yes,' he said. 'I learnt a heck of a lot about this place and the way it's run. Stuff I'd have been pretty glad to have found out twenty-four hours ago. But not one thing that helped over that damned problem.'

Into Ghote's mind there flashed once again, for the hundredth time, for the five hundredth, the dimensions of the damned problem. The big, bare room. Swami's body lying almost at its centre, the luxuriant black curls of his hair spread out on the close-fitting boards of the floor. That floor extending, clean-swept, to the bare walls all round. The yellow cushion-throne that was the sole object of any size in the room.

'Well, what did you learn in particular about the ashram?' he asked.

'I found out this much that would have been useful if this had been a straight investigation,' Lieutenant Foster said. 'There were just four people who knew that the Swami was not going to be in the Meditation Hall all night. There was first of all the Swami's Number Two, Johnananda so called. The Swami told him just before he began his meditation at 6 p.m. that he would go back to his own house at around 11.30 p.m. That must have been so as to be ready to meet me eventually, though apparently he didn't tell Johnananda that. But I had made my appointment with him around 5.30. All he said to Johnananda was he would be leaving the hall and wanted to see a girl called Emily Kanin, who acts as his secretary, half an hour after midnight. It seems he expected her full attention at whatever hour of the day or night he called for it. He was writing a book.'

'Yes,' Ghote said. 'I have met Miss Kanin, who prefers, she tells me, to be called Emily only. From her I have heard about that book, and from Miss Shahani also. It seems Swami expected very, very great things from it.'

Lieutenant Foster puffed out a sharp sigh into the surrounding air, minute by minute turning from dark to pale light. It was a sigh expressing a pretty sharp opinion of the Swami's book. An opinion that Ghote felt much inclined to endorse. But he persisted with the more prosaic matter in hand.

'There were four people altogether who knew of this intention to leave the Meditation Hall?' he asked.

'Yes. It seems Johnananda couldn't locate Miss Kanin—Emily—at first. But he came across her boy-friend, or her very good friend at least, a young man named Brad Lansing. And he asked him to pass on the message, in strict

147

confidence. I've interviewed him, and he swore that he told no one else but Emily and there's no reason why if he did talk to someone else he wouldn't tell me that he had. So that's two of them, plus Johnananda himself, real name John Richards, British citizen. And finally there's your Miss Shahani. She told me herself that the Swami had told her.'

'Yes, that is so. She informed me also. But, Lieutenant, did she tell you something else, something else about Swami?'

'What else? What do you mean?'

'Lieutenant, she told me she believes Swami committed suicide.'

In the slowly flooding-in pale light Ghote was able to make out now the cool grey eyes in the lieutenant's tanned face. They looked exceedingly thoughtful.

'Suicide?' he said. 'Well, of course I've thought about that. And it could be that the guy had some reason to take his life. If the Department's suspicions about what was going on here were correct and if we'd been able to get evidence of his sexual interference with underage girls, he'd have faced a long term in prison. Let alone public exposure.'

Ghote saw the unsmiling mouth in the taut, tanned face grimace suddenly in a rictus of distaste.

'But suicide or murder, Inspector, it makes no difference. Where's the knife responsible?

148

Where the hell is it?'

It was an unanswerable question.

But, Ghote thought, there might still be a way of perhaps getting towards an answer. If the Swami had committed suicide, then it was possible, unpleasantly possible, that he had used powers to move the weapon to some distant location that were on a much higher scale than anything he himself had been prepared to credit him with. The phenomenon was not unrecorded, by any means. If this was so, then any quest for the weapon was doomed to failure. But if it was not so . . . If the Swami had not committed suicide but had been murdered . . . Then there must be a way of finding the weapon. Because in that case it had certainly not been made to vanish by the use of supernatural powers. In that case there was going to be some logical explanation for its apparent disappearance. And that explanation could perhaps emerge, not by looking for the weapon, but by looking for the person who had used it.

'Lieutenant,' he said, 'I would like to question Johnananda. To question him without you being present.'

'Okay.'

There was a distinct note of resignation in the lieutenant's answer. It lingered in the dawn air. Until startlingly it was shattered.

'Attaboy,' Fred Hoskins exploded. 'That's the guy. We'll fix him but good.'

Johnananda did not make it easy for Ghote to
see him. But, Ghote reasoned, there was no
reason why he should. With the Swami's sudden
death Johnananda must be swamped with
business matters, even in the unbusiness-like
ashram. And then he himself had no authority
with which to demand an instant interview,
unless he were to give away the fact that he was
now actively co-operating with Lieutenant
Foster. And that was something he was
reluctant to do. It would deprive him of a
valuable advantage.

No, he had only the bare excuse that he had
come to the ashram at the behest of the father of
one of the disciples who was extremely anxious
about her. So he was content to wait till the early
afternoon for his appointment.

Not so Fred Hoskins.

'The guy's gonna make a break for it,' he said
to Ghote.

'But why should he be making any break? He
had not done so up to now.'

'Yeah, but that's because up to now he knew
he was only up against a straight cop. Now he's
gonna realize he's got a Hindu magic expert to
contend with.'

Ghote thought about trying, once again, to
get it into the huge private eye's jackal-fur head

that he himself was not a Hindu magic expert. And abandoned the thought.

'But why in any case would Johnananda wish to make the break?' he said.

'First of all,' Fred Hoskins answered, ticking off the point with one beef-red finger against the beef-red thumb of his other hand, 'the guy was second in command to the deceased and so he must be able to work the same kind of Hindu magic.'

Ghote thought of the orange-robed, shaven-headed Englishman, with his squeaky and unlistened-to reminders in the Meditation Hall. No, the man might manage to play the sitar after a fashion. But he was not someone with powers out of the ordinary.

'Go on,' he said.

'Second of all.' The beef-red finger moved to the beef-red finger next to the thumb on the other hand. 'In an investigative situation there is one question you gotta ask first. Now, what question is that, Gan boy?'

'It is the question that Dr Hans Gross expresses with the Latin words *Cui Bono*,' Ghote answered.

'All right. I'll tell you. It's the question: Who gets something out of it? That's what you gotta ask, Gan.'

'I see,' said Ghote. 'And you are thinking that since Johnananda was Swami's deputy he will inherit his place altogether?'

151

This did not seem to him a likely reason for seeing Johnananda as the murderer either. Whatever else there was to say about the Swami With No Name he had been a considerable personality. How else could he have had so many people, young girls, rich old women, boys, men, devoted to him? And Johnananda, Johnananda calling squeakily to the disciples in the Meditation Hall, was not a person with very much effective personality, if any.

'What other reasons have you got?' he asked.

'Third of all.'

The hulking private eye stopped abruptly and fell into thought.

'Well, there's plenty of other reasons,' he said at last. 'It's just a question of breaking the guy down. And you can do it, Gan boy. With your knowledge of Hindu powers you're bound to break down the guy's resistance. That is, if he's still there when you finally get that appointment he's been clever enough to delay making with you.'

CHAPTER TEN

Ghote was, however, not surprised to find Johnananda ready to keep their afternoon appointment in his office in the ashram's administration block, a room with its walls covered by radiant-coloured designs interspersed with pictures of the Hindu gods while the floor was occupied by Johnananda's large functional-looking orange plastic desk, a number of luxurious orange tweed-covered armchairs, a couple of smooth steel tables over which were scattered piles of clean, brilliantly white stationery and no fewer than three sleek electric typewriters and half-a-dozen calculators.

Ghote thought, with a pang of envy, how useful some of the items would be at his Crawford Market headquarters.

But this was no time for idle covetousness. Before the interview began there was a small, but important, matter to be arranged.

'Sit down, gentlemen, please,' Johnananda said, gesturing vaguely towards the tweed-covered armchairs set at a distance from his orange desk.

This was the moment. Ignoring Johnananda's gesture, Ghote snatched from against the wall near him a small plastic-seated office chair, tipped the little pile of pamphlets on it to the floor, swung it across and planked it down squarely opposite Johnananda and close up to his desk. To his delight, the quick manoeuvre paid off. Fred Hoskins subsided into one of the more distant armchairs.

Now, with any luck, the fellow would keep his promise not to intervene, extracted with some difficulty on their way back from the motel after a couple of hours' sleep on the gurgling waterbed.

For a long moment now Ghote looked at the man opposite him before attempting to ask the first of the seemingly innocent questions he hoped would lead him to finding out more about the first of the people who had known that the Swami would be in his house at the time he had died.

Yes, the fellow looked pretty well like a proper Indian holy man. His head was shaven, all but a tuft at the back. His eyes were deep-sunk in his almost fleshless face, indicating that the pleasures of the body had long since been abandoned. On his forehead was the spot of sandalwood paste most swamis put there, the spiritual eye as they called it. He was wearing his orange garments with obvious ease and familiarity. And he was sitting with that very upright back which was said to allow Kundalini, the serpent coiled at the spine's base in the subtle, spiritual body, to travel unimpeded to the brain. But, damn it, he was not a holy man, not a yogi. He could not be.

But all the same it might be clever to give him the respectful form of address a holy man was entitled to.

'Johanandaji.'

Johananda inclined his shaven head.

'Johnanandaji, I have been sent here, as you

154

know, by the father of one of Swamiji's disciples, Nirmala Shahani. Mr Shahani is very, very anxious about her welfare. Am I right, please, to understand that, now that Swamiji is no longer among us, you would be in charge of the ashram?'

Johnananda flapped a long-fingered hand over the scattered papers on his big orange desk.

'One doesn't like to go on about this,' he answered, 'but Swamiji had chosen one. Over the years, you know, one had made one's progress. However unworthy one is, one is one. And one must take up the burden that has been laid upon one.'

'Yes. And it must be a heavy burden, a heavy burden in material matters also, isn't it? All the land belonging to the ashram, that was in Swamiji's name? Does it all come to you now?'

Johnananda sighed.

'My dear fellow, if only you knew. The responsibilities, the responsibilities. Swamiji did make a will, you know, some time ago. By an awfully lucky chance one of the disciples here is a top, top lawyer, and he insisted that a proper will was vital. It seemed terrible, but money is money, you know, and land is land. And, do you know, the land here is even more valuable now than when it was given to Swamiji first of all? There was a change in the law, something I would never come within a million miles of understanding. But apparently the area can be

155

used now to build a senior citizens community on, only Swamiji—Well, oh dear, that's all got to be decided now by poor little me. With the help of the Ashram Council, of course. Only while Swamiji was here that never was much of anything, if you understand.'

'Yes,' said Ghote. 'I understand.'

He did. With the Swami With No Name at the head of affairs no democratic council was going to get a look-in.

'Tell me, please,' he added quickly, 'was this matter of selling the ashram's land what Swamiji was going to meditate on last night?'

Johnananda spread his long-fingered hands wide.

'That I just could not say,' he answered. 'Swamiji liked to keep a lot of things to himself, you know. And he simply hadn't told me what the problem was, just that he would spend all night in the Meditation Hall and then make an announcement at six in the morning. It might have been about anything. Anything. And in any case, as perhaps you know, he changed his mind and decided he would go back to his house. That was why it was there that he was found. well, you found him, as I understand.'

'Yes, yes. Yes, it was me.'

Here was dangerous ground. Would Johnananda want to know how it came about that he had entered Swami's house?

He shot out the first thing that came into his

156

head.

'I can see you are going to be very, very busy. There must be many other matters you will have to decide.'

'My dear chap, you have no idea. There's Swamiji's book. I mean, I gather from Emily who, for whatever reason she came here, really was a tower of strength to Swamiji, that there isn't anything like a manuscript. It's all just notes. Notes and jottings and ideas. So what is one to do about that?'

He looked at Ghote across his brightly smart plastic desk as if he hoped to get some firm literary advice there and then.

Ghote found he had nothing to offer. But he must keep this so usefully talkative fellow on the boil.

'Excuse me,' he said, lamely he felt, 'but I must ask about Miss Shahani. She had told that Swamiji was going to summon her to his house at some time during last night, though in the end he did not do so. Please, for what do you think that was?'

Johnananda's fingers flicked up into a wide, defensive fan.

'Now, I know what you're thinking,' he said. 'I know just what you're thinking. But, my dear fellow, I do assure you, you have nothing to worry about.'

'What worry is this?' Ghote said unyieldingly.

Johnananda gave him a tight, bright little

157

smile.

'Oh, let's not beat about the bush,' he said. 'It's the sex thing, my dear chap. That's what we're talking about, isn't it? That's what that very fierce policeman, Lieutenant Foster, wanted to see Swamiji about last night, isn't it? You see, nobody really likes the spiritual, especially when they know nothing about it. So they all want to pretend spiritual activities are something else. They prefer to think all swamis debauch little girls, my dear chap, rather than admit they might be giving them the greatest gift they could ever have, the gift of knowing where they were going. People hate that, you know. Hate it.'

Johnananda had spoken with growing, if shrill, vehemence. It drew a yet more vehement response.

Fred Hoskins rose from his low tweed-covered armchair like a waterspout suddenly spewing up in a placid ocean.

'Whaddya mean—hate? Are you accusing the citizenry of the Golden State of prejudice? Lemme tell you, California has a record second to none for its tolerance of all shades of opinion. Even Blacks and Mexes get a fair hearing here, provided they toe the line. You'd better cut out any more talk like that.'

Johnananda had been beating his long hands on the papers-strewn surface of his orange desk.

'But it's love,' he managed to get out at last.

'It's love that we at the ashram feel for everybody. We only want people to understand. That was what Swamiji preached: love and understand. And his message was getting through. Disciples have flocked here. My dear chap, flocked.'

'Yeah,' replied Fred Hoskins, still on his feet, looming tall. 'Yeah, they came flocking, right? And they came donating, too, yeah? Donating real heavy.'

'Really. Really, Mr—er— —er—Mr Hoskins, I don't see what that has got to do with it. Of course people gave to Swamiji. It was a sign of how much they respected and loved him.'

'And now you're sitting here hoping to cash in on that flow? You want to step into the Swami's shoes? To be on the receiving end?'

Johnananda's thin, fleshless face looked very pained.

'You don't understand,' he said. 'You just don't understand at all. Oh, good gracious me, I know that everything in the world is *maya*, illusion. I've long ago realized that. But I know, too, that I am here in what seems to be the real world, and the only thing to do about it is to act as if it was real.'

Fred Hoskins took a heavy step forward.

'You trying to tell me I'm not real?' he said. 'Because if you are let me tell you I'm gonna bust you on the nose.'

159

Ghote decided that it was time, high time, to cool the situation.

'Johnanandaji,' he said sharply, 'Mr Hoskins and I came here to inquire only whether you were the person now in charge of the ashram. We wished to speak to whoever could give us an assurance about Miss Nirmala Shahani.'

Behind him he heard with relief Fred Hoskins sink creakingly back into his orange tweed armchair. Across the desk he saw Johnananda, too, visibly relax.

He gave a little cough.

'Miss Shahani's father is most keen that she should return to Bombay,' he said. 'Can you kindly give me your full assurance that she is free to do so if she wishes?'

'But, my dear chap. Everyone in the ashram is free. They were free to follow Swamiji when he was here with us. They are as free to follow him through me, unworthy though I am. They are free to stay. They are free to go.'

Ghote at once got to his feet. He had already found out a good deal from what Johnananda had said. Now that Fred Hoskins had wrecked the atmosphere there was no point in remaining.

'Thank you, Johnanandaji. That is all we wished to know.'

He turned.

'Come along, Fred,' he said.

To his secret relief, Fred Hoskins simply lumbered to his feet and followed him out of the

160

office without a word.

But once they were standing out in the brisk mountain sunshine the belly-jutting private eye's attitude was swiftly reversed. He grabbed Gote by the arm.

'Gan,' he said, 'you let him go. You let him go when I had him running. It was a bitter disappointment to me that you handled that the way you did. If I'd had just two minutes more with the guy he'd have been down on his knees begging.'

'But what for would he have been begging?'

'Begging to confess. That's all, Gan. Just begging to confess to the murder of the man he planned to succeed.'

'I do not think so,' Ghote said.

Fred Hoskins drew himself up to his full height. Ghote was sharply conscious of the distance of more than a foot that separated that full, blood-pumped, jackal-fur-crowned countenance from his own. He had to make a strong effort to discount a feeling of being under a considerable disadvantage.

'Gan boy,' Fred Hoskins began, 'I would encourage you while you're on Californian soil to adopt an attitude of decent, honest-to-God aggression. You let that guy go, Gan. And you never oughta do that. Two minutes and he'd have been singing.'

'But what if he does not have anything to sing about?' Ghote answered as firmly as he could.

161

'We cannot even be certain that Swami was murdered. It may well be that he took his own life. What Johnananda had just said confirms that a little. He told that people hate what Swami claimed to give. So if a charge had been brought only that he had been violating your girls he would have been pilloried, you know. It is not beyond belief at all that he took his own life rather than face that.'

'I can't believe that, Gan boy. And let me remind you I've had a helluva lot of experience in these matters.'

For an instant Ghote toyed with the idea of saying something pointed about the experience of murder investigation likely to have been gained by a mere patrolman on the streets of Los Angeles. But he guessed that any such jibe would simply bounce off that rubber-plated exterior.

'Very well,' he said, 'let us leave aside the question of suicide and consider, if it is murder we have to deal with, who might have committed the crime.'

Fred Hoskins heaved in a great sigh. Like a schoolteacher contemplating his stupidest pupil.

'Gan boy, that John-whatsit guy is the murderer,' he said.

'It may be, Fred. But have you considered the position of Miss Emily Kanin also?'

'And who the heck is Miss Emily Kanin?'

'Miss Kanin, who prefers always to be called

Emily only, is the young lady who acted as Swami's secretary. But, as Johnananda has just revealed, she was something more than that also.'

'Yeah. That Emily. Well, I don't see what she's got to do with the case. Let me advise you about something, Gan boy. I don't know how you go about the business of crime detection in India, but here in the US of A, let me tell you, we get straight to the point. We don't mess around. We see a guy's got all the evidence stacked against him, we don't waste time with fancy notions.'

'Please, let me assure you that back in Bombay I am always only too happy to see who has committed a crime and to nab him straightaway,' Ghote said. 'But this is an altogether different matter.'

'Crime's crime, Gan boy. Just get that clear.'

Ghote restrained a sigh.

'Mr Hosk— Fred,' he said. 'This crime is a very, very different case from most murders. There is the matter of the weapon. Swami had his throat cut. I myself was on the scene within minutes only. There is no way out of that building except by the doors at the front, and I myself again and two deputies also were watching those doors. But the weapon that slit the throat was not there, Fred. And no one has been able to find it. That is what we have got to remember. That is why we must be always very,

163

very careful.'

Fred Hoskins put a heavy beef-red hand on to his short-cropped jackal-red hair and scratched his skull.

'Yeah,' he said. 'I guess.'

'So that is why,' Ghote said, 'we must be thinking now about Emily only.'

'Yeah, Emily. What's with Emily, Gan?'

'Just this, Fred. When Johnananda was talking about Swami's book he mentioned that Emily had been a tower of strength about it. But he said one other thing also.'

'I've gotta tell you that there you're wrong, Gan. Naturally I was paying close attention to every word that guy was saying. I'm fully aware of the importance of remembering every detail of a preliminary interview, Gan. And let me assure you the guy said nothing of any importance concerning that girl. He mentioned her. But that was all.'

'Well, he did say also something like: for whatever reason she was coming to the ashram. For whatever reason. Johnananda knew that Emily did not come here, however much she may have said so, because she was attracted to Swami. I believe, in fact, before she had been here long she did become attracted to him. I myself saw an expression of deep disappointment show itself on her face when she was forced to see that Swami was telling a lie. But when she arrived here first her attitude was

164

altogether different.'

'May be, may be. But it doesn't matter, Gan boy. Just compare it with the one hard fact we did find out in interrogating John-whatsit. That guy inherits, Gan. He inherits the whole darn lot. Don't tell me he isn't the one who did it, and, remember, he's got mystic powers. He admitted that. Came right out with it. Over the years, he said, he'd made progress. Progress in magical powers, Gan.'

'But he meant the ability to go into deep meditation only.'

'Yeah, deep meditation. A guy can do some very mysterious things when he gets deep into that. You know it, Gan. You've seen things that nobody in little old America would believe. And that's the way John-whatsit committed the murder. I know it. I just know it.'

'But, Fred,' Ghote burst out, hammered to a pitch of exasperation. 'Emily Kanin came here to the ashram for some secret purpose. We know that, too. And I think I know also what that secret purpose was.'

CHAPTER ELEVEN

It took Ghote and his lumbering, yammering shadow a good deal of searching to find Emily Kanin, spirit of the tennis-player, secretary to the Swami. But Ghote persisted, marching from place to place in the ashram grounds under the hot, clear Californian sunshine, patiently asking one dreamy, bemused, orange-clad disciple after another, young and old, boy and girl, plump matron determinedly forcing herself into something near the lotus position, bald-headed professional man with a rim of long hair caught up in a plait by a rubber-band.

The more he thought about Emily the more certain he was that she would repay investigation. What Johnananda had said about her was perfectly plain, and however feeble the fellow's claims as a yogi there was little doubt that he was someone who kept his eyes open to what went on around him.

No, Emily had clearly come to the ashram originally for some secret purpose. Just what that purpose was might be less clear. It might in the end prove to have no connection with the Swami's death. But some connection with the man it must have. There had been that other crumb of information Johnananda had let slip. A tiny fact, hastily suppressed.

It had been when the fellow had been talking about his many new responsibilities, about the decision that would soon have to be taken about whether to accept an offer made for the ashram's land by someone wanting to build a senior citizens community. That must be a project involving a very large amount of money. Americans at the end of their lives after years spent accumulating the riches of the world and seeking at last to enjoy that wealth, they would be ready to pay and pay for their comfort. So surely the concern seeking to build a retirement community would be willing to shell out a hefty sum to get hold of the ashram's suddenly available land.

But the Swami With No Name had not accepted their offer. Johnananda had let slip precisely this fact. It had been only in two hastily bitten-off words, but there could be no doubting their implication. Apparently, Johnananda had said, the area can be used now to build a senior citizens community on, only Swamiji—And then that abrupt halt.

However that sentence could hardly be completed other than with some such words as: only Swamiji had not agreed to the offer made.

But if the Swami had been holding out, whether for a better price or for some other reason, was it not possible, likely even, that people keen to acquire this suddenly available area of land would send some sort of a spy into the enemy camp? And what better spy than a bright, efficient young woman with high secretarial skill? She would only have to put herself and her abilities in Swami's way and he would be almost bound to make use of her. She had even admitted that this was what had happened. In the Meditation Hall when he had first seen her after Fred Hoskins had broken up the meeting with his piece she had said that Swami had 'just found out' that she had pretty good shorthand.

Just found out, indeed. Had her shorthand skill thrust under his nose, no doubt.

So, once established by Swami's side, she would be in a first-class position to discover his intentions about the ashram's land. She might even be able to influence him in favour of selling. And, if she had found she could not do that by a little subtle persuasion, then she would be in a position to see that foul means might work where fair had failed. That, for instance, a few carefully spread rumours about what Swami did with under-age girls could end by getting him out of the ashram in a hurry.

But, whatever Emily had had in mind in her early days at the ashram, once she had been close to Swami for a little time she had plainly fallen under his spell. What he himself had seen of Emily when Swami had told his lie about the car brochures, and later what he had heard from her, made that altogether plain. She had trusted

168

Swami. She had pledged herself to him. That was why his lies and his greed had so distressed her.

Distressed? She had been more than that. She had been struck to the heart.

So could it be that in her appalled disillusion she had at last tackled her idol, had gone to see him in his house earlier than the time he had requested her and had tried to persuade him back to the path he had shown her himself? And then a quarrel? And a snatched-up weapon?

But how to discover if this was what had in fact happened?

They tracked Emily back eventually to where they had first looked for her, in the little makeshift cottage with a fat black power-cable snaking up to its sloping wooden side that was her accommodation at the ashram.

Ghote knocked again at its roughly-made plank door. There was a moment's silence, and then Emily's voice called out a bright 'Come in, whoever you are.'

He pushed open the door—it had not even been properly closed, just resting against the door-post—and entered, Fred Hoskins ducking well down under the low lintel to follow.

The cottage was scarcely more than one large room divided in two by a pair of untidily crammed bookcases. In the back, smaller half Ghote saw a bed, old and sagging, with a couple of plaid rugs on it. In the front half the impression he got was more of an office than a living-room, despite a pair of cooking rings standing on the small, food-splashed table underneath the gingham-curtained window. On a larger table in the middle there was an electric typewriter—yet another—and several stacks of brightly coloured plastic-covered files.

The books in the bookcase, he saw as he completed his quick survey, were all works devoted to aspects of Hindu spirituality. He shied away from them.

And as he did so he realized something else that he had seen without immediately taking in. Emily was sitting in the room's only armchair—it had one arm broken in the middle—and on her lap there was a book. But it was lying at not quite the right angle for her to have been reading it when they had knocked.

It had been snatched, he was sure now, from the bookcase beside her. He stored the thought away.

'You're the visitor from Bombay,' Emily greeted him. 'The one who wanted to see Swami.'

'Yes, yes. And this is Mr Hoskins, Mr Fred Hoskins.'

'The guy with the gun.'

Yet the teasing, pleasant, oral-hygiene smile she gave them both as she said this seemed to Ghote to lack the confident radiance he had seen in her before. He was glad. If the girl felt

170

troubled she might be made to crack.

If there actually was anything for her to crack over.

'Miss Emily,' he said, putting a note of aggressiveness into his voice that would, he reflected, at least please Fred Hoskins. 'Miss Emily, I and my colleague here also, as you may know, came to the ashram on behalf of Mr Ranjee Shahani, of Shahani Enterprises, Bombay. Since Mr Shahani's daughter became a resident at the ashram she has failed altogether to communicate with her father and she has drawn out also the whole of a very large sum that was in a joint account at the State Bank of India, 707 Wilshire Boulevard, Los Angeles. Mr Shahani sent me to investigate the bona fides of the late Swami.'

While he had been speaking, banging out the words as if he was dealing with some pickpocket on the street of Bombay, Emily's face had from moment to moment taken on a deeper and deeper look of distress. Now she broke out.

'Listen, yesterday you told me you reckoned Swami had been lying when he said to Mrs Russell Walters he knew nothing about cars. I don't know how you got on to that, but I agreed then that he had. I agreed he wasn't what he ought to have been. But—Well, but—Oh, hell, I just don't know.'

Ghote made himself ignore her evident unhappiness, an unhappiness asking to be

171

comforted all the more because of the contrast it made with her overwhelming healthiness, plain in every inch of her tennis-player's body.

'Madam,' he said, 'you were very, very devoted to Swami, isn't it? But already before yesterday when I informed you that he had just told a most downright lie you were becoming doubtful, I am thinking. You knew in your heart he was not the seeker after truth you had believed. That is so, isn't it? Isn't it?'

'Yes.'

The word forced itself from lips that looked suddenly as if they had never been parted in a smile radiant with oral hygiene.

The girl looked up at him as he stood over her in the low, broken-armed armchair.

'I don't know what to think any more,' she said exhaustedly. 'I don't. I really don't. You know I came here, never mind why, fully determined that Swami wasn't about to have any influence over me. I didn't believe he could. I thought I really knew where I was in the world and what I wanted out of it. And—And then in one way or another I got pretty close to him. I mean, he kinda got to know I could take pretty fast dictation, and he wanted to use me for writing his book. And after that just being with him was enough. I was hooked, but hooked.'

She jumped to her feet and stood face to face with Ghote under the low ceiling of the little cottage.

172

'You can't tell me,' she said, her voice rising almost to a shout, 'that Swamiji didn't have some power, a power that people here in the West just can't attain. Or not unless they're like Johnananda and have been to India. But when Swamiji talked, when he dictated thoughts for his book, when he just sat there even, he took me with him into another world. You know, afterwards there'd be nights maybe when I was transcribing the things he'd said, typing up the actual words, and I'd look at them and think, hell, what's it all mean? It's just words, I'd say, words. Peace. Flowers. Action through inaction. Words, words, words. But when Swamiji was saying those words then, damn it, I saw. I saw a whole new world behind this grey, money-grubbing one. A world that would last for ever, a world that floated above everything.'

She turned away and looked down at the table with its bright plastic files and its sleek electric typewriter.

'Richer than rubies,' she said. 'It may sound just stupid, but that's what I felt. He showed me there was another world, richer than rubies.'

'And then you began to see signs of money-grubbing in him?' Ghote said. 'Of lies perhaps also? And at last came yesterday when he told such a lie that you could not any more refuse to believe he had said it.'

Slowly she turned back until she was directly facing him again.

'Yes,' she said. 'At that moment. And it hurt. It hurt then like someone was pressing a red-hot piece of iron into me.'

'Yes, I saw that,' Ghote said. 'But what afterwards, Miss Emily? Did you, when you knew Swami would be alone in his house, go there and punish him for that red-hot disappointment?'

He hoped for some violent reaction. He would have scarcely minded if it had been a screamed-out denial rather than a blubbered confession. The first might have meant as much as the second.

But he got neither.

Instead Emily dropped back sideways into her broken armchair slowly shaking her head.

'No,' she said, her voice muffled. 'No, it wasn't that way at all. I almost wish it had been.'

'What—What do you mean?'

Ghote felt offended by the seeming contradiction in what she had said almost as much as if she had spat at him from between her pearly, even, oral-hygiene teeth.

She looked up now, though her eyes were still clouded with doubts.

'If it had been that,' she said, 'if it had just been that I'd fallen for the guy's line, been carried away by a lot of talk and then had seen he was really only a greedy, power-seeking grabber dressed up in orange garments and I'd upped and killed him out of sheer rage, why,

174

then the situation would be something. I could have at least understood. But it isn't. It isn't.'

'It isn't? What isn't?

The eyes looking up at him smouldered abruptly with exasperated rage.

'Oh, can't you see? That knife. The weapon that cut his throat. It disappeared, didn't it? That lieutenant tried to fudge it over when he was questioning me but he couldn't. The knife that killed Swami wasn't there from almost the moment he died, and there was no way it could have been taken out of his house. So Swamiji is right back where he started from. The lies don't matter any more, if they ever did. He could do anything, couldn't he? Do anything?'

The rage died away, and the doubts returned.

'Only the lies do matter,' she whispered. 'They're still there too. Swami was not a good man. He behaved in a way that someone who was what he ought to have been could never have behaved. But—But even if he took his life for some reason or other, the way that he did it still means he was . . .'

What she believed the Swami With No Name still was, despite his lies and his hunger for the most expensive car California could provide, she left unsaid. Ghote did not need it spelt out for him. If that knife had been removed from the scene of Swami's death by means other than those that were to be found in the ordinary, material world, then the Swami was indeed a

175

yogi far advanced along the path and the manner of his death would remain for ever a mystery. And he himself sooner or later would have to return to Bombay leaving Nirmala Shahani behind, convinced.

'Well,' he said cautiously, 'I myself am still not certain that the knife was spirited away by supernatural means. Yes, I will admit that events occur in India that cannot be explained in logical, scientific terms. But I do not believe that Swami, whatever powers he might have possessed, was capable of achieving a feat of that kind. I am not certain even that he took his own life.'

Behind him, as he produced these decidedly unforceful and unaggressive thoughts, he could sense the bulky, looming form of Fred Hoskins making little, jerky movements as if small buried volcanoes were on the point of erupting from him.

If only the fellow would hold his tongue . . .

Emily smiled now. It was the palest replica of that flashing, pearly-teethed, cheerfulness-radiating smile that was her everyday self. But it was a mark of the sympathy that had begun to be established between them.

'I'd like to think the Swami I knew hadn't possessed extraordinary powers,' she said. 'I'd really like to. I'd know where I stood then. But . . . But you hardly saw him, did you? You couldn't have much idea of what he could do,

176

what he was. What it seemed he could do.'

'Well, you yourself watched him cure me of a very, very bad headache,' Ghote answered. 'And not just cure me only but see it also, my throbbing head, right across the Meditation Hall. I know what he could do.'

'Yeah, he did that. But you still think he wasn't really a true yogi?'

'I am still ready to carry on as if he was not,' Ghote answered. 'And perhaps you can help me to do that. For example, there is the matter of the senior citizens community.'

Emily gave him a quick, startled glance.

'You know about that?'

'Yes, I know about that.' He took a risk. 'I know all about it, Miss Emily. About what is involved and about the part you were playing also. You said just now that you came here first for never mind what reason. But I do mind. It was to act as a spy, isn't it?'

She nodded rueful agreement.

'It all seems a long time ago now,' she said, 'though it's really hardly more than a few weeks. But it seems years back to the person I was then. A girl with a hell of a lot of ambitions, and not too choosy about the way I got to them.'

'It was the best condo in the block, if I remember,' Ghote said. 'And, please, what is a condo?'

Emily gave him a glint of a smile.

'A condominium,' she said. 'It's an apartment

177

in a building owned by the people who live in it. It costs. But it means you have a pool and a gardener and a doorman, you name it. I wanted that. Once. And maybe I still want it.'

She sighed.

'I don't know, I just don't know any more.'

'And you were working for the company that is wanting to make a senior citizens community here?' Ghote asked. 'You agreed to come and pretend you were interested in Swami's teachings and then to—what was it that you said just now—let him kind of get to know you could take very, very fast dictation?'

'Yeah. That was it.'

'So, Miss Emily, I have to ask you. Who are these people you worked for? And what else would they do to get hold of this land?'

Emily looked as if she did not want to give an answer. But at last she spoke.

'I—I don't think so,' she said. 'I mean, it's kind of hard to believe. Okay, business is business and the real-estate world is probably as tough as any. And—And, well, the guy who runs the corporation, who is the corporation, is perfectly capable of playing rough to make a fast buck. But murder? Because that's what you're saying, isn't it? No, I don't believe murder.'

Ghote was aware once more of Fred Hoskins behind him barely suppressing a new outbreak of subterranean explosion. Hastily he challenged Emily.

178

'You do not believe it? But nevertheless you sound as if you do not think it is altogether impossible. Miss Emily, who is this man who is that corporation?'

Emily's lips, pink and full, were compressed into a hard, thin line now over her pearly lustrous teeth. But she answered in the end.

'He's a Mr Lansing,' she said. 'Mr Bradfield Lansing, Senior.'

'But—It is the father of your boy-friend? Your boyfriend, Brad? His name is Lansing. It is one of the few I have managed to find out in America.'

'Yeah, he's Brad Lansing. That's how we met, me working for his old man. But Brad's as different from his father as anyone could be. I used to think sometimes he was too soft. Too moony. He was into astrology and macrobiotics and organic gardening, a lot of stuff like that. Then—Then when I came up here and—And Swami ... Well, I wrote Brad and told him, and he came out too and in no time at all was just as excited about Swami as I was.'

'And when you began to think Swami was a liar? What then, Miss Emily?'

'Nothing. I didn't say a word to Brad. I—I somehow didn't want to.'

'Yes, I can see that. And he never knew? Never guessed about your doubts?'

'I don't think so. I'm sure not. If he had, he'd have come right out with it. Brad speaks before

179

he thinks too much, and always has.'

'Yes,' Ghote said. 'He did that in the Meditation Hall, isn't it? He said what came into his head, and Swami humiliated him for it in front of everybody.'

'Yeah. But that isn't . . .'

'That isn't what, Miss Emily?'

She looked at him with a spurt of defiance from down in her low broken chair.

'That isn't what you're thinking. Brad would never have resented anything Swami said or did. However humiliating it was. Brad knew some people have to take that sort of thing from their guru. It's the path for some people, and Brad was one of them. He didn't go to Swami's house last night and take it out on him. That's what you were thinking, isn't it?'

'But he did know that Swami would be there,' Ghote said. 'He was one of only four people who knew that. He was rebuked by Swami in a very, very brutal manner. And another thing, Miss Emily, however different he may be from his father, he is his father's son. His son and heir, isn't it? With that same name? So if his father makes a very, very big profit, that profit will come to the son one day. Isn't it?'

CHAPTER TWELVE

They left Emily angry. She had reacted in rage to Ghote's taunting hints that it might well have been Brad who had killed the Swami. He had hoped that anger would cause her to blurt out something, either about Brad or herself, that would take him a step forward. But her denials had all be unsupported by any facts.

It had not even been very easy getting from her where Brad might be found at this time. At last, pearly teeth flashing in rage, she had flung out at them that he would be on duty at the Visitors Centre. Ghote, manoeuvring the towering bulk of Fred Hoskins in front of him, had hurriedly left.

Together they made their way through the ashram's central circle towards the long dirt road leading down the hill. There were two deputies standing on guard on the steps of Swami's extraordinary spiralling-roofed house. Their hands were resting on the butts of their pistols and they looked not at all happy.

But Ghote refused to let himself be impressed by that. There was nothing in that building for grown men nervously to finger guns about. The man who had died there had not lost his life in any way different from the forms violent death ordinarily took. He had not. He had not. No mysterious spirit was going to attempt to rush in on the scene of that death. Neither was one going to come roaring out, impervious to heavy bullets.

This was a murder, or perhaps a suicide, like any other. It must be.

Evidently, however, the sight of the two deputies had caused a massive train of thought to surface in Fred Hoskins's jackal-fur-topped head.

'Gan boy,' he said suddenly, laying a beef-red hand on Ghote's elbow and bringing him to a halt in the passageway between Swami's house and the dining-hall, just beside the half-mended bicycle that had so cheered him by its happy Indian-ness the first time he had set foot here.

'Yes, Fred?'

'Gan, it is my duty to inform you of a certain fact.'

'Yes, Fred?'

'I want you to know, Gan, that working alongside you, a foreigner and a member of an alien race, here in God's own country, I realize that I have a very great responsibility.'

'Yes, Fred.'

'Gan, I am going to suggest you now take a fresh look at this whole case.'

'Yes Fred?'

'Yes, sir. It's become clear to me that you're heading in the wrong direction. I didn't tell you before in case it might reflect on the skills and methods of the Bombay police force. But I feel it's my duty now to let you know my opinions.'

'Yes, Fred.'

The huge private eye drew himself up to his greatest height. He plunged his thumbs into the wide black leather belt that cinched him in under his grain-sack of a belly.

'Inspector Goat,' he said, 'The person responsible for this case of Murder One is a man we already know. It's not that clean-living girl we've just interviewed.'

Ghote broke in. He knew as he did so that it would be useless. But some irrepressible prickliness in him produced the words before he could check them.

'Fred, I have never said it is Miss Emily that we are looking for. Fred, at this moment I am on my way to talk to the young man, Brad, a person we have yet to interview.'

'I regret to inform you, Gan boy, that you're mistaking my intentions. That's probably natural in an officer not accustomed to the operational methods of the Californian police forces. But you still don't understand.'

'I am sorry, Fred.'

'I accept that apology, Gan, in the spirit in which it was given. And let me tell you I honour you for it. A man who has the intestinal fortitude to apologize when he knows he's in the wrong will always have the respect of Fred J. Hoskins.'

'But Fred, you were saying . . .'

Why could the fellow not get on with it? If they were going to go on standing here like this lecturing and receiving lecture the business that reared up in front of him like a malignant, wide-spreading kikathorn hedge would never be beaten down. And, he suddenly realized, he held a conviction—had it only just been born in his head?—that there was an answer, a logical answer, to it. The riddle of Swami's death did have a logical solution, however improbable it might prove to be. And weren't the improbabilities human beings were capable of creating all too probable in any case?

If only he could just get on with the business of seizing hold of all the necessary facts.

'I was about to tell you, Gan, exactly why you're going in the wrong direction. Point Number One: the Swami was murdered. Point Number Two: he was murdered by one so-called Johnan-something-or-other. Point Number Three: the murder was carried out by means entirely alien to us here in the West. Point Number Five: those means only you understand, and what you've got to do is concentrate on bringing these unAmerican methods to light.'

For an instant Ghote thought of asking what had happened to Point Four. But instead he embarked, feeling himself pushing uphill an immense stone juggernaut wheel, on explaining

184

how matters stood in his own estimation.

'Fred, we have found nothing at all to prove that Johnananda killed Swami. He is only as much a suspect as Miss Emily, or I regret to say Nirmala Shahani. And we have begun to see that Brad Lansing is perhaps more likely than any of them. Besides, also it is not at all impossible that Swami's death was suicide.'

If we could forget that knife that is not there, he added to himself.

But he saw from the fixed expression planted on Fred Hoskins's big, beef-red face that all his explanation had been time wasted.

'Gan, it is very likely because of your unfamiliarity with our American way of speaking that you didn't understand the most important words uttered by that sweet kid in your presence a few minutes ago.'

He wished violently that he could snatch up the bicycle beside him and pedal off at full speed out of any chance of hearing anything more from this yammering giant of obstructiveness. But the machine's front tyre was still dangling loosely round the wheel, its inner tube missing. This was not a time for miracles.

'Yes, Fred,' he said. 'What is it I have not understood?'

'I will quote you her exact words, Gan. I owe you that. And you will want to thank me for the remarkable accuracy of my memory.'

'Thank you, Fred. Already.'

'These then were her exact words: There are certain mysterious powers possessed only by Hindu Indians plus also certain individuals, namely John-whatsit, who have had the opportunity of extensively visiting India. That was what she said, Gan.'

Or not unless they're like Johnananda and have been to India. Yes, Emily had said that. And it was true that, though the words had struck him, he had thrust them aside in his eagerness to follow the trail he had seen opening before him then. It could be, too, that the words were important enough. At the least they went clean contrary to his own opinion of Johnananda as a weakling Englishman making a poor attempt at playing swami.

Yet even if Emily's assessment of Johnananda might be more accurate than his own, blinded as he might have been by prejudice, did it mean that the Englishman was any more a likely suspect than he had been before? Did they show, those words, that Johnananda had killed the Swami by supernatural means? Clearly they did not go as far as that.

He drew in a sharp breath.

'Fred,' he said, 'I have noted your opinion, and I would agree that those words of Miss Emily's that you so accurately remembered had escaped my full attention. But, nevertheless, if only for the sake of elimination, I am now proceeding to interview Mr Bradfield Lansing,

Junior.'

And he proceeded. He turned on his heel and marched off at a rapid pace over the softly springy pineneedle-coated ground.

But Fred Hoskins followed.

'Gan, I want you to know that I appreciate what you're doing. You're using the process we call elimination. You're cutting out, all the possibilities, no matter how wild, before we home in on your target. That's good thinking, Gan boy.'

Ghote, marching down towards the Visitors Centre and Brad Lansing, decided he was not going to offer any thanks for the compliment.

Fred Hoskins, long, meaty legs striding out, kept pace with him at his shoulder. And, pouring steadily on to his unprotected head, there came an unending waterfall of clacking noise.

He tried the use of mental discipline to shut it out.

'So you'll have all the necessary information, I'll give you a rundown on the principle of the retirement community, a system that's been developed in the Golden State to a point where no other place can rival it. You know why I'm giving you this info?'

'Because you believe Johnananda killed Swami to gain large financial benefits,' Ghote snapped, his mental shield having proved unavailing.

187

'The reason is so you realize that Johnan-
something murdered his predecessor in order to
cash in.'

'Yes, Fred.'

If only the fellow would stop. If only it were
possible to be quiet and think. There must be
questions to ask that, if put correctly, would
bring to the forefront of his mind the answer he
had suddenly felt that deep-down he already
knew. Perhaps some of those questions he ought
to be putting in just a few minutes' time to
young Brad. But even trying to think what they
might be just now was like attempting to light a
match while tumbling headlong down a river in
full monsoon spate.

'I guess in India you don't see many
retirement communities. Don't get me wrong.
I'm not criticizing the Indian way of life. It's a
way you people have chosen, and you have to
stick with that choice.'

'No, Fred, we do not have retirement
communities.'

We are more sensible, he wanted to add. We
keep our aged family members with us in the
home. Where they enjoy being, and where we
honour them for the age they have attained,
where they pass on to us and to our children by
the mere fact of their presence the knowledge of
life and the wisdom that has come to them over
the years.

Instead, he tried lengthening his stride. The

sooner he got to the Visitors Centre the sooner this battering downpour of words would cease.

But Fred Hoskins's long legs had no difficulty in keeping him right at his elbow.

'When a man has come to the end of his working life, Gan, what he wants to do is play all the golf he never had time for when he had to worry about making enough money to be able to play golf whenever he wants. Not only golf, but bridge and canasta, tennis, or bowling even. Any or all of these are available to the retired person. Now, I'd like you to get this clear in your mind: a man doesn't want to play golf if he's gonna be interrupted by jerks with beer cans or by people of, ah, different racial origins from himself. That man wants peace. It's his right.'

There came a pause. But Ghote knew that making no comment would not prolong it.

'Yes, Fred,' he said.

'So enterprising real-estate corporations buy up big lots and build houses. Mansions, sometimes, equipped with every convenience to make life as comfortable and carefree as possible. Such corporations have naturally also included assets like swimming pools, golf-courses, tennis-courts, country clubs, restaurants, shopping centres and radio stations. And they've set up private peace-keeping forces and their own private undertakings to provide such signs of respect as the motor-cycle escort

189

for the cortege.'

It took Ghote some few moments to grasp from the unfamiliar word cortege just what this last phrase of Fred Hoskins's deluge had meant. When he did so there flashed into his mind a picture. There was a raggedy procession of chanting, music-making mourners behind a two-pole bier on which, draped in white with face exposed and garlanded, lay the body of his own father on its way to the burning ghat, and the return of its exhausted flesh to the common matter out of which over the years it had been made.

But he shook the image from his mind. He had a task in front of him. Brad, the disciple he had seen humiliated by Swami in front of everybody, how was he to approach him?

From over his shoulder the clacking word-splurge poured on.

But at last the Visitors Centre came in sight.

Ghote flung a question back towards the looming private eye.

'Fred, do you wish to be present when I am interviewing this young man?'

'Yes, sir, I most certainly do.'

In sudden silence Fred Hoskins followed him into the round, log-walled building. Its racks of floaty orange garments, its glass-fronted cupboards with their arrays of electronic meditation timers, folding meditation benches and yoga pants (made in India) seemed at once

190

familiar and from some far distant time, a time when he had been no more than an innocent seeker of a perhaps captive girl, deeply worried about how he would be able to cope with the giants who surrounded her and their wily master.

Now, however, instead of being empty of people, something that had momentarily encouraged him when his throbbing head had been all too unprepared to tackle even an ogre's outrider, there sat at the central eight-sided table Bradfield Lansing, Junior, orange T-shirted, orange trousered, legs encased in clumping green rubber boots.

'Oh,' Ghote said, pretending surprise, 'here is the very person I was wanting to meet.'

Young Brad looked up.

'Me? You wanted to meet me? I guess I don't exactly know who you are.'

Ghote smiled. Ingratiatingly.

'No, no, you would not at all know me. My name is Ghote. I am from India. From Bombay. I have come here actually at the request of the father of one of the disciples. He is very, very worried about what has been happening to her.'

'I wouldn't think he's any cause to worry. Anybody at the ashram couldn't be in a better place.'

'A better place?' Ghote let a pause hang for a moment. 'Well, but please excuse me, only yesterday I was seeing what Swami did to you.

191

That did not look very good to me.'

A smile, a grin, lit up the boy's long, intent face.

'Hey,' he said, 'you got the wrong idea. An ashram isn't a place you go to have yourself a good time. It's a place you go to find you're having a better time than you ever knew you could.'

From behind Ghote's shoulder the massive form of Fred Hoskins stepped forward.

'Say that again,' he demanded.

Brad blinked.

'This gentleman is Mr Fred Hoskins,' Ghote said with haste. 'He is my American colleague.'

Almost he added: two thousand rupees a day plus expenses.

'Oh. Hi, there,' Brad said. He blinked again. 'Let me try and explain it another way. What a true guru has to give to a *chela*, a disciple, eventually is bliss. But he doesn't just deal you out a ration of it just because you come and ask, or maybe pay. No. He shows you the path. He makes you see how the whole materialistic bag is weighing you down. And, then, if you can follow him, in the end you get there and find you've attained bliss.'

'There?' said Fred Hoskins, with deep suspicion. 'Where's there?'

Ghote wondered what it would take to shut the fellow up. If Fred Hoskins was going to engage in debate about the nature of the spiritual life, especially when he seemed incapable of viewing anything other than from his own crassly materialistic point of view, they would never get to the point of putting this young man under pressure. They would never get him to reveal, possibly, that he had been in the Swami's house the night before. They would never learn, the secret of what had happened to the weapon that had cut Swami's throat.

Brad's young, intent face took on a yet more serious expression. His eyes rested on Fred Hoskins's beef-red countenance gravely as a judge's.

'There,' he said. 'You ask where's there, and you've got every right to ask. But I can't tell you. I know an answer exists. I know it here.' He thumped his somewhat narrow chest. 'I know it. I'll tell you: Swamiji utterly changed my life from the moment I got here. He made me happy, completely happy. I have all kinds of moods, but I'm always happy now.'

Quick as a mongoose darting at the neck of a writhing snake, Ghote jumped in.

'Happy?' he said. 'And were you still happy when Swami was hitting you yesterday? Was that a step on your path to there?'

Brad's eyes lit up.

'Yes,' he said. 'Yes, you're beginning to see it. A guru has to show you the way. For some he does it with love, if that's what'll get rid of the mind-chatter they're full of. But for others he does it in other ways. Maybe by slapping them like yesterday, maybe even by putting them through a hell of a lot worse.'

Again Ghote saw a slim gap where he could dart to something else he wanted to know. Again he jumped in.

'A girl. If a guru is wanting to stop—what was it?—the mind-chatter of a girl, would he do worse to her than slap only?'

Brad stirred uneasily on his orange plastic-seated chair. He looked hard down at the spread of glossily bright pamphlets on the table in front of him.

'I know why you're asking,' he said.

'Yes,' Ghote answered. 'I am asking because of things I have heard. I have been sent here, you know, by the father of Miss Nirmala Shahani, who is very much fearing what has happened to his daughter.'

Brad looked up at him with pained eyes.

'I don't know,' he said slowly. 'Jeez, how could I know? For certain know? I mean, if Swamiji ... Well, if Swamiji did use to break girls' pride by, well by practically raping them, they wouldn't want the whole world to know. And they shouldn't either. What happens between a person and his guru, if it's in private, it's private.'

'But,' said Ghote.

He thought that this one word would be enough. It was. Brad looked down at the table

194

again, shuffled a pile of pamphlets together, then hastily spread them out once more.

'There's always rumours,' he said, his voice little more than a mutter. 'In a place like this there shouldn't be, but some of the kids...'

Ghote, standing close beside the boy and doing his best to make his body into an implacable wall to which no answers but the truth could be offered, saw the thin, bare neck bent over the bright spread of the pamphlet-strewn table.

Some of the kids, he thought, echoing Brad's words. I am looking at a kid now, however near to man's estate he is.

But he was not going to allow himself to let the boy off the hook, however much sympathy he might feel for him.

'Well,' he asked, riding Brad down with every harsh syllable, 'just what was it that some of the kids used to say about Swami?'

The honest, serious eyes turned to look squarely at him.

'They said Swami used to do it, used to have some of the girls.'

'That he used to ravish girls? But these rumours and tittle-tattles, did they say also why it was that Swami did that? Did they say it was to break spirits only? Or did they say it was for his pleasure?'

Brad flushed. Hot, ashamed blood in the pale cheeks of his long, serious face.

'It was only rumours,' he said, his voice rising. 'Just simply rumours. They shouldn't have been saying such things. They shouldn't have been thinking them even, not here in the ashram.'

'Nevertheless,' Ghote said, not loosening his grip by the least amount, 'there is the saying "No smoke without fire". What was the fire that made that smoke? Tell me.'

'I don't know, I don't know,' the boy answered, in something near a wail. 'There— There was a girl. Patsy Warren. She left.'

Suddenly he pushed back his rich orange chair and got to his feet. He turned, clumsily in his heavy green rubber boots, and addressed the far wall of the circular room.

'As a matter of fact,' he banged out, 'she left just as soon as she'd seen what happened to me yesterday afternoon. I guess she was ready to quit anyhow, and what she saw seemed to be the last straw for her. She got it all wrong. She thought it would happen to her, and—And, from what some of the guys said, she added that on to what Swami had done with her already. Done to her. Done to her, if you want.'

Ghote made a guess.

'She was a girl who wore a white pullover? A white rollneck pullover not altogether clean?'

'Yeah. That sounds like her all right.'

'And you say she left? Yesterday afternoon?'

A thought had come into his head. Here was

196

somebody, somebody at last, who plainly detested the all-loved Swami With No Name. Could it be...?

'Yes, she left. As a matter of fact I took her to where the Greyhound bus stops. She was heading back for New York, where she came from. Said she never wanted to see California again.'

A small disappointment. Back to the situation as before.

Ghote sighed.

'You saw her entering the bus—that is a long-distance bus, isn't it?' he asked, as a last formality.

'Yeah. We were only just in time. I helped her on with her cases. She didn't even wave goodbye.'

'But she had told people here, definitely, that Swami has ravished her?' Ghote asked, ignoring the pathos.

'I don't know if she exactly said that. But there were guys happy to make out that that was what had happened. Some people are purely malicious.'

'In spite of hearing Swami every day? In spite of all that he was teaching?'

Ghote had put the questions only because, to his secret pleasure, the discovery of purely malicious disciples at the ashram had reinforced his own views about the Swami, views he had not always found it easy to go on believing.

197

Brad turned to face him now, shaking his head.

'You can't expect a guru to jell with everyone who chances to come by,' he said. 'Not even the highest yogi going could do that. But I tell you this again: for me Swamiji was the most mind-whammy thing that's ever happened. For me he was.'

Ghote noted the fact of the boy's sincerity. Yes, the Swami had had some powers. Despite the malice that lingered in others of his followers.

'But however mind-whammy the Swami was being for you,' he said, unable to keep a little bitterness out of his voice, 'he still could not take away—what was it you said to him in the Meditation Hall?—that lump of greed in you. Come, tell me the truth, you are still in the grip of that greed, isn't it?'

And, to himself he added: you are still capable of helping your father make his extra million by buying the ashram land, and capable perhaps of lashing out with some weapon—what weapon?—if your betrayal of Swami had come to a head somehow.

'I don't know. I tell you I just don't know.'

Standing there, a really rather ridiculous figure in his orange T-shirt, floppy orange trousers and lumpen green rubber boots, Brad flung out the words in evident desperation.

If only the boy were not wearing those

198

damned boots. If only his feet were visible, and his toes. Those give-away, curling-up toes. Then when the questions came raining down on him, so thick and fast his mind could not grapple with them, then that tell-tale sign might be there.

And the answer to what had happened to that knife be not far behind.

But, feet visible or not, he must do what he could to break this breakable creature in front of him.

He began.

'Your father, you told your father what they were saying about the Swami and girls. Isn't it?'

For lack of toes he was keeping his eyes firmly fixed on the boy's Adam's apple. Many men were unable to prevent a tell-tale jerking there when they had important lies to put over. But Brad's throat showed no betraying sign, and his voice when he answered seemed to be filled only with surprise.

'My father? What's my father got to do with all this? I don't understand.'

'Your father is very much wanting the land the ashram has,' Ghote said. 'I think you are knowing that. And knowing also that Swami refused the offer your father made. So, if your father could create a big enough scandal, he could force the Swami to leave.'

'But that's ridic—'

The boy stopped suddenly.

'Emily,' he said slowly. 'Was that why she left Dad's office and . . . But, no, she couldn't. She wouldn't.'

'Yes,' Ghote said, pile-driving the word in. 'That was why your Emily came here. But then she started to believe in Swami, and she stopped sending your father the information he was wanting. So then when your father heard that she had written to you about Swami he sent you out here as his spy. That is so, isn't it? Yes? Yes? Isn't it?'

'No,' Brad shouted, eyes rolling wide like a trapped horse's. 'No, no, no. You don't understand. You don't understand at all. My father—My father's just the plumb opposite to everything I am. He—He never thinks of anything except the money he can make, and the smart deals and the next million.'

'And you? Don't you ever think of those millions also? All this talk about liking the life of the ashram. You can afford to like it. You know that whenever you want you can go back to your father and his millions and the comforts and the luxuries he can offer.'

'But I don't. I—'

'No wonder you were ready to help him make yet one more million out of the land here. No wonder.'

'No.'

The boy's cry rang through the circular room. Ghote acknowledged in silence that it truly

200

seemed a genuine cry of horror at his suggestion. Yet if the boy had in fact killed Swami would he not lie and lie and lie again about it?

He looked down in rage at the lumpy green rubber boots.

CHAPTER THIRTEEN

Outside, when Ghote had exhausted the remainder of his rain of bouncingly useless questions, he told Fred Hoskins that he wanted as soon as possible, this very afternoon if time would allow, to see Bradfield Lansing Senior.

'The kid's father?' Fred Hoskins at once objected. 'Now, listen to me, Gan boy, that's not the way this crime is going to be solved. It's going to be solved by you proving to Lieutenant Foster just how that knife mysteriously disappeared from the Swami's house. And let me tell you this: you're going to do that only by pinning the murder on that guy Johna-whatsit.'

Ghote saw an immense steep hill rising up in front of him. He felt a dragging weariness.

Till a sudden inspiration banished in an instant both ever-rising hill and all fatigue.

'A process of elimination, Fred,' he said. 'You yourself were telling me that a process of elimination is the *modus operandi* of the Los

Angeles Police Department. I wish to see Mr Bradfield Lansing, Senior, in order finally to eliminate his son from the inquiry.'

'Right on, Gan boy.'

Ghote received a tremendous slap on his left shoulder. With stoical calm.

'You see, Fred,' he went on, nervously explaining a little more than he need have done. 'I was not at all able to decide whether young Brad was telling the truth. If he was not—and I am certain that he is still feeling the sensation of greed within himself—then it is certainly not impossible that the Swami was murdered because of this land deal.'

'But, Gan boy, if it's just a matter of deciding whether the kid was lying, there's a real easy way of telling.'

'No, I do not think so, Fred. Yes, you can look always for signs of tension that a person does not know he is making. But it is difficult to know that when a person is a good liar. Sometimes the most honest person can lie very, very much better than a thorough miscreant. It is a question of how much they are feeling justified.'

'No, sir. I got to tell you that you're way off base.'

What was this? What had the fellow got into his head now?

'Well, I shall hear what you have got to say, Fred, with much interest.'

'It's just this, Gan. We here in the State of California have eliminated once and for all the question of lying and truth-telling.'

Ghote wanted to say: I don't believe you. Instead he remained silent.

'There are many police forces in the world, as I understand it,' Fred Hoskins declared, 'who don't take advantage of the invention of the polygraph. And I'll bet that the Bombay force is one of those institutions.'

'Well, yes, Fred, it is. It must be. But, please, what is this polygraph?'

'The polygraph, known familiarly to us in the LAPD as the poly, is an infallible electronic device which shows by monitoring the witness's blood pressure whether or not they're telling the truth. It's as simple as that.'

A boiling fury at once filled Ghote's head. Such an infallible machine could not exist. It must not exist. Something that took away from human beings their sacred ability to tell lies was not to be thought of.

In his anger he could scarcely sort out exactly why it was that the thought of this—this polygraph so outraged him. But he was certain that it did. It seemed to him—only surely Fred Hoskins must be lying himself, or at least have got the details of the device all wrong—that to have such a mechanical way of dealing with the whole many-sided part of life that truth-telling and lying, half-lying, white-lying and black-

203

lying constituted would be to deny a whole aspect of man's will. Let alone taking a lot of the joy out of crime detection.

For several seconds he could think of nothing to say. He stood there in the sunshine outside the Visitors Centre looking straight to the front, to just the point where Fred Hoskins's boldly coloured plaid shirt was open at the neck to reveal the top of a chest pelt of jackal-red hair, and he let the rage run and run in his head.

At last he managed to get calm enough to say a few cautious words.

'That is most—most interesting, Fred. Very, very interesting indeed. But—But I am wondering . . .'

'You have every right to wonder, Gan.'

Ghote drew in a long breath.

'Well, what it is I am wondering, Fred, is this: why if such a marvellous machine exists, why hasn't Lieutenant Foster been making use of it throughout this case?'

His question did seem to set the hulking private eye back a little.

'I—I guess the good lieutenant has his own reasons,' he said at last. 'I'm not the man, Gan, to cast doubt on the methods an officer of Lieutenant Foster's standing decides to employ. That's something each and every officer must decide for himself. And now I suggest you get down without delay to the LA headquarters of the Lansing Realty Corporation, a building I'm naturally familiar with.'

'Yes, Fred.'

★   ★   ★

The drive back to Los Angeles in Fred Hoskins's huge green car was, to Ghote's mind, like sitting watching a film he has already seen being run through again backwards. And, since they were anxious to reach Bradfield Lansing's office before he left at the end of the day, much faster.

The same out-of-this-world freeways swept and swooped through the country, splitting sometimes into two separate highways one in each direction and almost far enough away from one another to be going to different destinations. The same extraordinary procession of vehicles came thundering towards them or were overtaken by Fred Hoskins's aggressive driving. There were the same enormous double tankers thundering along at sixty or seventy miles an hour and containing—was Fred Hoskins really to be believed about this?—milk. Or perhaps now, towards evening, empty of milk. There were the same extraordinary halves of houses being transported entire, coloured curtains flapping at their windows. There were great open trucks filled to the brim, six, eight or ten feet deep, with tomatoes or with grapes. There were the same mind-deadening road-signs. *Speed Checked by Aircraft, Eat All You Want.*

It was the repetition of a nightmare. Only this time there was one difference. For some reason Fred Hoskins seemed to have run out of talk. The monologue about the beauties and magnificence of California, which on the way out to the ashram it had been possible to muffle only by pretending to be asleep, was no longer on offer.

But it was replaced by music from the car's four-speaker stereo radio. At first Ghote had welcomed this. Under the blare of sound, he thought, he would be able to concentrate on the business of the Swami and that damned knife, he would be able to tease from his mind the facts he felt convinced were layered away somewhere there. He would learn the answer.

Yet within a few minutes of Fred Hoskins reaching for the button on the car's immense dashboard that had brought this torrent of noise upon them he realized that it was preventing thought every bit as effectively as the huge private eye's customary outpouring of hectoring information.

And not only was there the music, there were the frequent interruptions for advertisements as well. If anything, these were more disruptive of quiet, logical thought than the blare of strident song they interrupted.

Clean, healthy-looking skin starts here. To be really beautiful your skin must first be scrupulously clean. That's why our Skincare Ritual includes washing with one of our special soaps. Discover the beautiful difference. Visit our specialist in your nearest great store, trained with care to understand your skin, its problems and how to solve them. Meet with her soon and begin a lifetime of clean, healthy-looking skin.

Surreptitiously Ghote stroked his left cheek and examined his palm afterwards. He had sweated a little in the brilliant sunshine. Did his face show it? Would he have clean enough, healthy-looking enough skin to face a top Californian businessman?

He tried once again to get straight in his mind just what he needed to find out from the top businessman that would fit the puzzle he sensed lying almost completed down below a level of his mind at which he could reach it.

But the thunder of the four separate sound streams from Fred Hoskins's speakers once more battered thought into submission.

Let us plan your party the way you dreamed it would be. Start by sitting down with our professional party consultant. He'll show you how to set the mood, create the theme. How to find the right caterer, the right florist. Party big or celebrate small, we have what you need to turn a common variety party into sheer unadulterated fantasy.

Ghote screwed up his eyes in simple misery. Hadn't he already found enough fantasy in this materialistic America?

He wondered if keeping time to the beat of the new onrush of music would help to chase away thoughts he did not want. The experiment failed.

Most of all you need a Fashion Kitchen. A kitchen the ultimate expression of your personality and lifestyle. Find the look that is really you among our wide array of stylings from period traditional through today's contemporary. We invite you to come browse.

Should he, before he started back for Bombay—With a wiser and sadder Nirmala Shani? Or, alone, and sadder himself?—should he go browse there and perhaps find something, some small intimate expression of a lifestyle, to take back to Protima? And would it, whatever it was, however much today's contemporary, make up enough to her for that pilgrimage to Banaras, promised but indefinitely postponed?

More music, blotting out everything. Other advertisements. *Is your dog a picky eater?* And others. *Thinning hair problem? Have real hair added one strand at a time back into your own.* And then the outskirts of mighty, spreading Los

Angeles.

And smog again.

The bare hillsides had given way to rows of bright, staring stores, all to Ghote's eyes in extraordinary good states of repair. How often they must be painted and re-painted, he thought to himself. And how big even the smallest of them was, at least twice the size of the narrow dark shops that crammed the streets of Bombay. And how often these Los Angeles stores must be knocked down and rebuilt to look so new. What energy there was here. What confidence. It made Bombay's pushfulness, famed all over India, look like the mere excitement of a bad dose of fever.

He sat in silence beside his enormous, jutting-bellied companion intent at the wheel of the monster car, slipping easily from one traffic stream to another, only occasionally over-riding the strident continuing stream of music with a scornful comment on some other driver, a woman or the possessor of a number-plate from outside California.

The huge, boldly-painted store names presented themselves to his battered-at mind, hung there vibrating for a moment, vanished.

Jack's.

Pete's.

Simon Platt.

Bill Green.

Each was enormous, high, high in the air.

209

Proudly flaunting. And the joke names, too. They commanded you to laugh, and to buy, by the very brightness of the paint in which their huge, inflated letters were written.

Leaning Tower of Pizza.

Grime Does Not Pay.

Give A Dog A Good Mane.

Nine Billion Unsold Sandwiches.

A vision of these last, toppling mountain upon toppling mountain of bread, occupied him until he realized that they had come into a street seemingly entirely dedicated to the car. Stores advertising, in huge letters, mufflers (which he felt proud to recognize as silencers). Salesrooms by the dozen. Gas stations in cheek-by-jowl competition. Stores devoted to selling car insurance. Stores advertising Hot Wax that made him realize how polished almost all the cars in California looked. How different from the dust-smothered vehicles, and the carefully hand-washed ones, of Bombay. How often these Americans must clean their cars. No, have them cleaned. At the car-washes everywhere. At the Hot Waxes.

German Car Center. A whole place devoted just to selling cars from one distant country.

He closed his eyes and shook his head gently from side to side, as if he could induce this last assault on his mind to slide off without lodging there to add to his sense of being obliterated, overwhelmed.

'Our trip took exactly one hour and twenty-seven minutes. We're in good time to wrap up this elimination process, return at maximum speed to the ashram and conduct our final interview resulting in the arrest of one Johnan-an-an.'

Fred Hoskins's boom recalled him to what lay ahead. The hammering music had abruptly ceased.

He looked out of the huge car's ever-closed windows. They had slid to the kerb outside a tall glass tower of an office block. By ducking and twisting his head he could see it climb and climb into the smog-greyed sky.

And not five yards away at the side of the glossily impressive marble portal of the building there was a large brass plaque on which were incised simply the two words *Lansing Realty*.

Ghote felt a sickening sense of opportunity wasted. He had been sitting with nothing to do in the car for exactly one hour and twenty-seven minutes and he had failed altogether to bring his mind to bear on the problem that lay like a great ironstone boulder across his path, the mystery of the missing knife. He had allowed Fred Hoskins's music to beat him.

He was not even ready for the interview that lay ahead.

'Fred,' he said, succumbing to a temptation, 'you have made very, very good time, but are we too late? Will Mr Bradfield Lansing be here to

211

receive us?'

'It is not even a quarter to five. An American business executive will still be at his desk.'

Was that really so? There were Bombay businessmen who came to office at half past ten in the morning, left early for lunch at the club, came back from lunch late and were soon away again, heading for the golf-course. On the other hand, there were other Bombay businessmen, those whose offices were often no more than a low-ceilinged room above a small factory or at the back of a shop, where under creaking fans they spent hour after hour from early morning to late at night at their cash-books.

Were all American businessmen, in contrast to this diversity, as total slaves to designated office hours as Fred Hoskins had stated? Perhaps when they entered this great glass tower of a building they would find out.

Already the fellow was out of the car.

Ghote hastily scrambled to join him on the sidewalk. He felt yet more unready to tackle the real-estate tycoon.

'Fred,' he said, 'even if Mr Bradfield Lansing is at his desk, why would he consent to see me?'

The mountainous private eye turned towards him.

'Gan boy,' he said, 'you have the privilege of being accompanied by a licensed private investigator of the State of California. A California businessman, I assure you, will

212

appreciate the work carried out by the licensed private investigators of the State. He'll give us an interview.'

He will not, Ghote said to himself in a spurt of perverse rebellion. I will take a bet with myself that we do not, just because Fred Hoskins is a licensed private eye, get to see the head of Lansing Realty.

'Yes, Fred,' he said. 'Shall we go in?'

Side by side they climbed the broad steps to the massive entrance, passed through its tall, opened aluminium doors, walked across a lofty lobby and took the elevator to the thirtieth floor—How swift, how silent it was. Did it ever have a notice on it saying *Out of Order?*—where, it appeared, Lansing Realty's particular share of this great glass tower began.

When they got out they found themselves in another lobby with behind a long black marble reception-counter a girl sitting, one long leg crossed over the other, as impressive and antiseptic as the polished stone in front of her.

Fred Hoskins marched across, took out his wallet from his back pocket, extracted from that a large white card, scrawled a few words on it and asked the girl to send it 'at your earliest convenience' to Mr Bradfield Lansing, Senior.

A little to Ghote's surprise the girl, when she had glanced at the card, picked up the pale green telephone at her elbow and spoke urgently into it in a deliberately low voice. He wished he could make out what she was saying.

But he was not left long in suspense. He had not had time to reach the long leather sofa on the far side of the lobby when the girl's voice, loud and clear now, broke the softly humming silence.

'Mr Lansing will see you directly. His personal office is at Floor 35.'

So he had lost that wager with himself. An American business executive, it seemed, was to be found at his desk until the very end of business hours, and a licensed private investigator of the State of California did have some divine claim to obtain an interview on request.

Fred Hoskins had been right.

CHAPTER FOURTEEN

The man's office was overwhelming. Ghote, in its doorway, was for a moment unable to take a step forward. He stood, convinced for that fraction of time that he had been transported back through all the hours of his long, disorienting flight from India to California and that he had been physically displaced, too, from Los Angeles back to Bombay.

Displaced to an overwhelming office at the top of a tall building where, as here, a man sat

214

behind an immense carved, dragon-disporting desk separated from the door by two vast carpets, light in colour, ready to be smirched at the touch of a shoe, fields as well for the writhing play of guardian dragons. To an office where, as here, the walls were all window and the windows were concealed by pale slatted blinds themselves half-hidden by rich green foliage lushly growing in great earthenware pots or fat sagging baskets.

He pulled himself sharply together. No, he was in Los Angeles, conducting an inquiry on which perhaps his own career depended and which was going to end, must end, in the exposure of a diabolical trick.

Yet, despite the fact that the man in the tall, studded chair behind the huge desk bore a distinct resemblance to young Brad Lansing, he almost said to him. 'Good afternoon, Mr Ranjee Shahani, sir.'

But Fred Hoskins, Fred Hoskins who had triumphed in predicting the ease with which they would get this interview, was already trampling forward over the first of the two huge pale carpets. Ghote made sure that by the time they had reached the great glossy dragon-writhing table-desk they were marching shoulder to shoulder.

'Mr Lansing,' Fred Hoskins boomed as they arrived, 'you already know who I am and also, no doubt, the fact that I am here with

215

information concerning your son, Bradfield Lansing, Junior. I am here to tell you he is deeply involved in the case of the murdered Swami, with which you will be familiar from your hourly news bulletins.'

Brad's father—that look-alike face, Ghote saw now, was fired by a different, tougher seriousness and was leathery-dry where his son's was pale—looked at the tall, belly-jutting detective with shrewd, hard eyes.

'Mr—er—Hoskins,' he said. 'I can give you just three minutes. What is it you have to tell me about Brad?'

'What I have to inform you of,' Fred Hoskins replied, not at all subdued by his reception, 'can best be communicated by the gentleman I have brought here with me.'

He swung round to Ghote.

'Mr Lansing. I have the honour to present one of the most eminent investigators in the Indian hemisphere, Inspector Ghote, of Bombay, India. He is collaborating with myself and the Los Angeles County Sheriff's Department in the solution of the case in which your unfortunate son is mixed up.'

'Inspector?' Bradfield Lansing said, a note of considerable respect for such police top brass showing itself in his voice. 'Inspector. Well, I am extremely glad to meet you, sir, and even to hear you're interesting yourself in my hippie son.'

Ghote decided he would not divest himself of the dignity Fred Hoskins had brashly bestowed on him.

'Mr Lansing,' he answered, rounding out his tones as much as he could, 'you are busy and I would try not to keep you long. But it is true, as you have heard, that your son is possibly under suspicion of murder. So if you would be so good as to answer a few questions for me, it would undoubtedly assist him.'

The long, leathery face on the far side of the huge, gleaming carved desk took on a plainly sour look.

'I don't know whether I'm prepared to go very far to get that hippie out of a hole. He's opposed me in everything he could since he was thirteen years old. I've told him he was going to hell, and now he's there I'm not so sure he shouldn't stay.'

'But, Mr Lansing, he is your son.'

'Right. He is. My only son. But, goddammit, I'd rather see every cent of all this—' A swift wave of the hand embraced huge table-desk, sombre gold cigar-box on it, dragon-sporting carpets, green jungle-tapestry of houseplants, the whole tall glass building. 'All this, go to the State of California, when I pass on rather than into his pockets.'

'Mr Lansing, tell me please, is your son aware of the sentiments you have expressed?'

Brad's father gave a little grunt by way of a

217

laugh.

'If he isn't,' he said, 'it's certainly not my fault. And he's often enough had the cheek to tell me he doesn't want any of my money. What's money for, I ask you, if not to hand on to those that bear your name when the day comes. Long may it be.'

'Yes, sir,' said Fred Hoskins with enthusiasm.

'But, Mr Lansing,' Ghote put in quickly, 'have you any proof of what you have said?'

'Proof?' The hard eyes in the leathery, long face considered for an instant. 'Yes, sir, I've proof enough if you need it. I've had that conversation with the boy in front of his mother. I've had it here in the office in front of my secretary. I've even had it in front of the Mex servants. Mr—Mr Whatever-your-name-is, that boy is mad. Mad and bad.'

'So there is no question,' Ghote said quietly, 'of your having asked him to assist you in securing the land upon which the ashram stands?'

'There is hell—'

Bradfield Lansing brought himself to a sudden halt. Ghote caught one sharp, shrewd look in his eyes. Then he saw him draw in a long breath.

'Inspector,' he said at last and very slowly, 'I guess I don't altogether understand what it is you're driving at. How come, for instance, you

218

have such a particular interest in the ashram? As I recall, the—the guy in charge there was killed less than twenty-four hours ago. Has the Indian Government got some special concern about the case? Have they had you flown out here already?'

Ghote cursed inwardly. If Bradfield Lansing was going to challenge his right to ask questions he would not have a leg to stand on. And if the necessary questions were not put, then the prospects of clearing up the mystery of the Swami's death would be solidly blocked.

What to do?

He was still hesitating when an unexpected ally came crashing to his side.

'Mr Lansing,' Fred Hoskins clattered out. 'Inspector Goat is in close collaboration with myself, and I am, as you are aware, a licensed private investigator of the State of California.'

'So the girl in the front office said,' Bradfield Lansing answered, his face unmoving.

But Ghote saw, his right hand slid along the underside of his huge carved desk. It was a fair bet that it had touched a concealed bell-push.

'Yes, sir,' Fred Hoskins was saying, 'a licensed investigator. And I am in process of investigating a matter of the very gravest importance, so I would be greatly obliged if you would answer my questions.'

Bradfield Lansing's eyes rested on him for a moment. Then he spoke.

219

'Well? What questions do you have?'

Fred Hoskins drew in a massive breath.

'I—I would like to ask—That is—That is, I prefer these questions be asked by my Hindu colleague, Inspector Goat.'

'And if I'm not willing to answer questions from a person with no standing in the matter?'

'Then—Then—'

But Fred Hoskins was saved from finding a fearful enough penalty for such a response by the sound of the door opening at the distant end of the enormous office.

Bradfield Lansing's secretary was there.

'Mr Lansing,' she said, cool and efficient in every syllable, 'it's time for your Jacuzzi.'

Ghote failed to understand the meaning of the sentence. But he very well understood why it had been said. Bradfield Lansing, under expected pressure over his land deal at the ashram, had secured his retreat.

And, with that realization, a sharp and angry determination jetted up inside him. There were questions he must ask this man, questions that very well might clear a path through to a solution of the intolerable mystery that confronted him. He was not going to let those questions go unasked.

'Mr Lansing,' he said, 'I am not at all understanding what is a Jacuzzi, nor how important it is that it cannot wait. But there are matters which you must answer. If you do not

220

answer them to me now, then you will have to answer them to Lieutenant Foster of the Los Angeles County Sheriff's Department later.'

The long face only a shade paler than its background of the tall, glowingly polished leather chair looked at him in silent thought.

'You're collaborating with this Lieutenant Foster, are you?'

Ghote guessed the question was asked more in order to stall for time than for information.

'Lieutenant Foster has requested me to give him such assistance as I am able to,' he said firmly.

'Yeah.'

Bradfield Lansing fell silent again.

Ghote looked him straight in the eye across the expanse of his huge, swirlingly carved desk.

At last the realtor moved a little in his tall chair.

'Okay,' he said. 'You want to ask me questions, I'll listen. If it saves me a session with the Sheriff's Department I'm happy. But I really do have to get into that Jacuzzi pretty soon. Will you join me?'

'Please, what is this Jacuzzi?' Ghote said, not restraining the suspiciousness he felt.

Bradfield Lansing had slipped out of his imposing chair and was coming round the big desk to them.

'Come and see for yourself, Inspector,' he said. 'It's up on the roof. We'll take my private

221

elevator.'

Without waiting for an answer he set out across the two enormous dragon-covered carpets. Ghote paused an instant and then followed him.

A minute later they were out on the roof.

At once Ghote realized that they were above the level of the smog. Warm sunshine struck on his shoulders and he looked up to see a sky of deep, delightful blue.

Whatever a Jacuzzi might turn out to be, he felt immediately, he would be able to cope with it. However evasive Bradfield Lansing might prove, he would be able to pin him down eventually.

He looked around him more carefully. About half the roof, he saw, was taken up by the mechanical contrivances necessary for any tall building, great belching air-ducts, blank-walled shapes, that no doubt housed elevator motors and water tanks. But the other half of this sunshiny out-of-the-world area was devoted to sport and leisure. There was a pair of high-meshed tennis-courts and a small swimming pool. And there was an enclosure surrounded by a tall wooden fence towards which Bradfield Lansing was leading them.

Rising above the palings Ghote saw wisps of steam. The realtor opened a narrow door and went in. Ghote and Fred Hoskins followed.

Inside there were wooden steps leading in a

gentle spiral to a wooden platform in the middle of which there was a little pool about six or eight feet across, its sides made of heavy redwood. The clear water filling it almost to the brim was steaming vigorously.

'Here you are, Inspector,' Bradfield Lansing said. 'The Jacuzzi or hot tub. Come on in.'

Was there a hint of malice in the hard eyes in that long, leathery face? Ghote could not decide.

But the real-estate tycoon was already stripping off his clothes and dropping them on to a narrow wooden bench running round the inside of the enclosure. And Fred Hoskins was peeling off his bright plaid shirt and carefully laying his piece in its holster under the bench.

It was plain that if Bradfield Lansing was to be questioned effectively it would have to be done in the tub. To stand over it while the fellow lolled in its hot water and bend down and shout out what he wanted to know was obviously not a practical possibility.

But that would mean taking off his clothes. All his clothes.

Well, if that was what was necessary to get the answers to his questions, so be it. If this was all that lay between him and the eventual solution of the mystery of that disappearing knife, then it was a small price to pay.

He sat on the bench and rapidly removed his shoes.

Bradfield Lansing and Fred Hoskins were a

little ahead of him. Each, as soon as he had stripped, sat on the edge of the steaming pool and then slipped into its clear water. Ghote saw the huge private eye's skin, milk-white where it was not normally exposed to the air, turn instantly scarlet.

He pushed down his underpants and, feeling absurdly unprotected, hastily stepped up to the poolside, sat and dropped his legs into the water.

It was fiendishly hot.

But Bradfield Lansing was in it up to his neck and his long tanned face wore a slight smile. Was it sensuous pleasure, or was it delight at having manoeuvred an enemy into an awkward position.

Ghote gritted his teeth, did his utmost to plant on his features an expression of calm, even of mild boredom, and slid downwards.

Immediately he felt his body buffeted by a strong underwater current, live and lithe as a heavy snake. It pushed him to one side. Another similar current struck him and pushed him back. The twin flows, and others from other angles, brutally beat at his flesh already within seconds softened and made swollen by the heat of the water.

He felt humiliated. A catspaw.

'Well, Inspector, you like it?'

Bradfield Lansing's long face was beaded with sweat, but it seemed to Ghote as it came floating up close to his own, to wear an expression of something like triumph.

'Yes,' he answered firmly. 'It is very, very hot but I am liking it. Yes.'

'Guaranteed to smooth away all the cares,' Bradfield Lansing said, pushing himself backwards.

'All the cares?' Ghote asked sharply, fighting inwardly to regain his mental balance. 'You have many, many cares then, Mr Lansing?'

'I have my share. But that's what being in business is about, I guess. You want to make money, and wanting that's what makes the world go round. So you hit on some way you can do it. And then you worry about doing it more and better. That's okay: the worrying makes you work harder than the other guy.'

'And now you are worrying whether you will be able to buy the ashram land?'

But the realtor did not seem put out by the question as he had been when it had first been shot at him down in his huge office.

'I guess you know that that guy, that swami, if that's what you call him, was holding out on me for a better price?' he asked.

'Yes, I know that.'

'And the lieutenant from the Sheriff's Department, he's interested in that fact too?'

'Yes,' Ghote said with firmness. 'He is thinking it is a matter than should be very much looked into.'

225

One of the heavy water-jets sent him willy-nilly close up to the long-faced realtor. He made frantic movements of his outstretched hands to propel himself back.

'Well, you tell him whatever I tell you. I've got nothing to hide.'

Ghote found a footing on the redwood bottom of the little pool and kept pushing till he was at a reasonable distance from the subject of his extraordinary interview. How had he allowed himself to be trapped by the Californian way of life like this?

'You have nothing to hide?' he asked. 'Not Miss Emily Kanin even?'

The eyebrows of the realtor's long face rose in acknowledgement of a hit. But it was the merest acknowledgement only.

'Was it you or was it the lieutenant got on to that?' he asked after the briefest of pauses.

Fred Hoskins, plunging forward and sending a whalelike wave of steaming water slopping over the edge of the tub, took it on himself to answer.

'I am happy to inform you that it was my distinguished colleague here who, with myself, made that discovery,' he said.

The sweat-dripping leathery face in front of Ghote did not turn away.

'Okay, yeah. I put the girl in there. I wanted to see what she could find out about the set-up. Maybe I hoped she could prod that guy in the

226

right direction.'

'To prod him?' Ghote said. 'Perhaps to prod him to death? Isn't it?'

He had never banged out the tough question to a suspect in circumstances so absurdly wrong. But he judged that the moment had come and he made his voice as unyielding as if he were back at Crawford Market headquarters and had some bemused wife-murderer in front of him at maximum disadvantage.

The long, sweat-shiny face backed away a few inches.

'No, sir. You're wrong there. Business is business and, damn it, I'll go to the very edge of what's legal to win on a deal, and cheerfully, too. But to murder a guy to get hold of some land, even one hell of a lot of land worth a bundle? You must be crazy.'

'But your son,' Ghote pursued, sensing that for all the man's denial he himself still held the advantage, 'would your son seek to increase the family wealth, which could still become his, by resorting to murder?'

Two long, leathery hands appeared above the surface of the steaming water and beat at it.

'I've told you, sir, and I've told that boy often enough. Not one red cent of mine will he get till I see he's ready to make some honest money.'

'But, Mr Lansing,' Ghote thinking of young Brad kneeling in front of Swami taking his slaps, felt obliged to say. 'Your son is not an

227

anti-social. He is by no means any sort of miscreant.'

'I guess he's not. But he's doing no good to himself or anybody else, the way he's been acting these last five years. No, sir, a man has got to do more in this world than moan about how bad it is. A man's got to work. He's got to make himself some money. To build something that wasn't there before.'

'By getting hold of valuable land by means of underhand methods, Mr Lansing, must he do that?'

Let him have the naked truth, Ghote thought. He has tricked me into this naked confrontation, so let him have the worst of it as well as the best.

But the long, sweat-beaded face in front of his showed no sign of being disconcerted.

'Underhand methods, Inspector? Well, I just don't know what you mean by that. You can't mean I've done anything illegal because Lansing Realty has taken damn good care never to go one step beyond what the law allows. You can examine the books any time you want. But if you mean tough methods, well, I make no apology for using those. It's a tough, world, Inspector, and if you don't stand up to it and fight it you go under. But if you can take the world on its own terms, then you stand to come out of that fight with a few dollars in your pocket, and what's more you leave the world a

228

better place to be in. You've made something, and you can be proud of that. No, sir, I've got nothing to apologize for, and don't you forget it.'

Inspector Ghote took one quick breath and plunged his whole head under the scalding water of the Jacuzzi.

CHAPTER FIFTEEN

Back in Fred Hoskins's monstrous green car, Ghote admitted to himself that at least he felt a good deal the better physically. He felt comfortable in every inch. Freed, too, of all minor cares.

But this latter was a state that lasted only until Fred Hoskins had started the car's deep-throbbing engine and had begun to pull out into the heavier-than-ever evening traffic.

'Okay, Gan boy, we're hot on the trail now,' he said, his voice bouncing back at Ghote from the roof overhead, the wide windscreen in front of him. 'Let me tell you here and now I wasn't impressed with your theory that a take-over of the ashram land had any direct bearing on the case. A simple business transaction doesn't lead to first-degree murder, Gan boy. Maybe in Bombay, India, where they have a different attitude about money these things happen. But let me assure you in the Golden State our business ethic prevents those sneaky tactics. No, Gan, it's that Britisher in the orange you've got to concentrate on from here on. How did he use the mysterious ways of the East to make the murder weapon disappear? That's what I'm counting on you, Gan, with your know-how, to make one hundred per cent clear.'

'But,' Ghote had just time to reply before the jackal-haired private eye reached for the button that set off his quadraphonic loudspeakers, 'but, Fred, there is the question of Nirmala Shahani still. She also knew that Swami would be alone in his house, remember.'

And, he added to himself as the first blast of music struck his ear-drums, Nirmala Shahani is all now that stands between me and admitting that Swami took his own life and was alone responsible for the disappearance of the weapon. Because the interview with Bradfield Lansing, Senior, if it had done nothing else, had cleared his son of the last vestiges of any reasonable suspicion. The young man would not inherit his father's wealth, had no interest in that wealth and well knew how matters stood. And, equally, it had been clear ever since their encounter in the Visitors Centre that the boy in no way resented Swami's brutal handling.

So Brad was out. And so was Emily. For one thing, if Lansing Realty was not prepared to step one inch outside the law to attain its ends, and the offer to open the books for inspection would seem to validate that, then Emily could never have got into a situation where she might have been accused of spying or worse and then have lashed out and killed Swami. But neither had she killed him for another reason. She had gone to the ashram in the first place as a spy, though no more than a simple spy. Then Swami, with that gift he undoubtedly had had for winning people over, had claimed her. Until she had begun catching him out in lies. From then on she had been in two minds about him, even after that final lie up on the Meditation Hall platform. And no one in two minds, he said to himself, has crude will enough to kill.

Which left, of the four who had known where to find Swami at the crucial time, only Nirmala and Johnananda. And Johnananda, Fred Hoskins's choice, was just not the man for murder.

Let us correct your figure problems—easily, simply, painlessly, without wraps, shots, pills or machines. Call today for your Free Body Analysis.

The hectoring, fourfold voice, almost as mind-deadeningly burdensome as Fred Hoskins's own, broke in on his thoughts. He tried to get back to the train of logic that he believed he had begun on. But now he could no longer resist the thump-thump-thump of the battering music as the fantastic eight-lane

231

freeway began to reel out in front of them.

What is gin? Gin is a state of mind. Only Bombay Gin imported from England . . .

Bombay gin? Had that really been what that arrogantly confident smooth voice had just thundered out at him? And if it was Bombay gin—Oh, what would he not give to be bumping along a mere four-lane road out of Bombay at this instant—then why did it have to be imported here from England? He would never understand this place. Never.

And, besides, had he not known all along that the answer to the riddle of that missing knife would not come at the end of any logical process beginning with the elimination of young Brad and of Emily? It was in his head already.

But how to get it out? How? How?

Treat yourself and your friends to the luxury of a luscious champagne breakfast served to you at your home in bed by Golden Egg Express.

No. No. No. No.

'A trip of under one hour thirty-six minutes, and if that crazy woman in that toy-car Volks with the Oregon plates hadn't cruised along in the middle of the highway at fifty miles per hour I would've beaten my best time yet.'

'Yes, Fred.'

The central circle of the ashram buildings was there again, the big white dome of the Meditation Hall, the extraordinary spiralling roof of Swami's house. And the mystery as

232

unsolved as ever.

But there was still something to be done, still part of the logical process not gone through.

He pushed open the great green car's fat door and set his feet on the firm, reddish earth. Then he addressed Fred Hoskins over the huge width of the car's hood.

'Fred, Lieutenant Foster has been good enough to ask me for whatever assistance I can render. And I am going to give him that assistance, my own assistance. I shall go now and find Miss Nirmala Shahani, and when I have done so I shall interrogate her in a certain way. I do not altogether want to do this. But I must. And I will.'

He had, tucked away in a corner of his mind, a tiny hope that such a declaration would send the towering private eye off away in an almighty rage. Not to have that insistent presence looming over him. Not to hear that yammer-yammer-yammer about the Californian way of life. Or, worse, about the Hindu way of life. Not to have, even when the fellow was silent, the feeling that at any instant there would come a geyser-burst of words spattering out at him till every sense was numbed. Not to have to carry this giant one single inch further upon his shoulders.

To be able to think.

'Gan boy, I have to tell you that you're failing to take into account one very important factor.'

233

That Johnananda is the killer. Yes, Fred. For the good and sufficient reason that he is both a Britisher and a mysterious Hindu at one and the same time. Yes, Fred.

'Oh, yes, Fred? And, please, what factor is that?'

'You've failed, Gan, to take into account the activities of Lieutenant Foster and the vast resources of the Los Angeles County Sheriff's Department. In our absence, Gan, it's very possible that the case has been solved.'

'Yes, Fred,' Ghote said, coming thumpingly down to earth. 'You are right.'

He hoped the fellow was indeed right and the answer to the intolerable mystery known. Or, he discovered, analysing that hope, he knew that this was what he ought to be feeling. Nothing but satisfaction that those huge mechanical and electronic resources had done their job. But, because there at the bottom of his mind was the belief that he himself had known what that answer was before even they had left for their zooming, speeding trip to Los Angeles, he had wanted the pleasure of producing the answer, of flourishing it even, first of all. He wanted to have been the one who had proved that this was not an impenetrable mystery but something simply subject to the laws of science and logic as everybody understood them.

But if the lieutenant had found the answer then good luck to him after all.

234

'Fred,' he said, 'we must ask. We must ask at once.'

He set off for the log-built administration block at a run.

Yet he hardly needed to get inside and knock at the door of the office Lieutenant Foster was using to know that whatever had happened in the Swami's spiral-roofed house at around midnight was still baffling the best resources of Californian crime science. The very deputy on guard in the central corridor of the building, a bored, resigned figure, told him everything.

'Come in,' the lieutenant called.

He was sitting at the desk in the office, an impressively wide affair made of stainless steel, and the mere sight of the piles of papers on it confirmed Ghote in his knowledge that the case was no further forward. He had found himself at the same stage of affairs often enough in Bombay. That time in the progress of a difficult case when fact upon fact upon fact had been discovered, committed to bureaucratic paper and dumped in front of the investigating officer. Sometimes by diligently going through every such recorded item it was possible to come across a discrepancy or something small but significant that had been overlooked in the first excitement. Then, sometimes, an answer might emerge. More often, though, all the labour was in vain, the many accumulated facts said nothing, any discrepancies meant nothing.

235

But the job had to be done, and he felt a sense of warm comradeship now to see that the grey-eyed lieutenant had been methodically working from one stacked pile of papers to another.

'There is nothing new?' he asked him.

'There's one hell of a lot new, Inspector, but not a darn thing that helps so far as I can see.'

'Yes. I am sorry to say that so far I also have discovered nothing that is helpful.'

The lieutenant looked up at him. His unsmiling tanned face was drawn with fatigue.

'Tell you one thing may be you hadn't thought of,' he said.

'Yes? What is that, please?'

'Haemophilia, Inspector.'

For an instant Ghote could not think what on earth the syllables meant. Then it came back to him, from one short aside in a Police College lecture of long ago. That curious disease—it had had something to do with Victoria, Queen Empress—in which the blood does not clot.

Good God, had Swami suffered from that and . . . ?

'Didn't have it,' the lieutenant said laconically. 'They checked at the Lab in Sacramento.'

And you asked, Ghote thought with admiration. You asked.

But Lieutenant Foster only pulled down his mouth resignedly.

'No, it's the weapon,' he said. 'There's just no

236

getting away from that.'

Ghote almost burst out then with his belief that there was a rational solution to that mystery, and that he knew the answer. That it was somewhere in his head.

But he stopped himself. What use would it be to say he knew the answer if he then would have to add that he could not lay his finger on it. It would be very, very unprofessional.

Lieutenant Foster sighed.

'By the way,' he said, 'at least we know now what the weapon was.'

Hope sprang up in Ghote like a wavering, delusive flame of marsh-fire.

'What?' he said. 'What is it? How did you . . . ?'

'A razor,' the lieutenant answered wearily. 'An old-fashioned razor, the kind they call a cut-throat. The criminalists at Sacramento have been looking at the photographs. They're sure. And I'm not about to question their findings.'

'No. No, if that is the scientific answer I am happy also to accept it. An old-fashioned razor? Well, I suppose it is very likely that the Swami had such a thing in his bathroom. I did not see anything of the sort when I was there, but I saw the bathroom for a few seconds only.'

'You were right, though. There was no razor there. But that guy Johnananda confirms that the Swami had such a razor. Apparently he often got to shave the guy with it himself. Mark of respect from disciple to guru, he told me.'

'Yes, yes. That would be so. But, Lieutenant . . .'

'Yeah?'

'It seems to me, I must say, that knowing just what the weapon was does not actually advance us at all.'

'You're right, it doesn't,' Lieutenant Foster said.

'You're wrong, it does.'

Fred Hoskins's jutting grain-sack of a belly was protruding through the open doorway.

He stepped further in.

'No, Gan boy,' he continued, booming like a loud-hailer, 'I gotta inform you you're making a real boner there. The weapon that killed the Swami was a razor, right?'

'Yes, you have just heard.'

'And the man who used that razor on the Swami's cheeks who was he, Gan boy?'

'You have heard also,' Ghote said with exasperation. 'It was Johnananda. But—'

'But nothing, Gan. I've mentioned the name of that guy in a negative connection before, and what I've just heard confirms my instinct that there is the perpetrator of this crime.'

'You've talked with Johnananda, Inspector?' Lieutenant Foster said.

'Yes, I have. And while I cannot state beyond doubt that he was not responsible for the death of the Swami, I do not find it easy to believe he

238

killed him simply in order to inherit his position.'

'That makes two of us, I guess,' the lieutenant said.

Emboldened by this definite support, Ghote put a question he had wanted to ask the lieutenant since just before their dash to Los Angeles.

'But, please, tell me, Lieutenant, did you when you questioned Johnananda make use of a device that is called, I believe, the polygraph?'

A tiny smile lifted a corner of the lieutenant's weary mouth.

'It has its uses,' he said. 'But don't get to thinking it's the only answer. A pathological liar won't show up on it—not that I think Johnananda's one of those. And there are guys who can beat the machine without thinking about it. Guys with their blood pressure under control, I guess. And maybe that description does fit our friend.'

The tribute to Johnananda, if it was a tribute, surprised Ghote a little. But he was prevented from pursuing the subject.

There was a bellow from just behind him.

'I tell you I can spot a no-goodnik at fifty paces, and that guy—'

'You want another crack at him, Inspector?' Lieutenant Foster cut across the protestations.

'No,' Ghote said. 'No, it is not Johnananda I am wishing to talk with. It is somebody else, and this is a matter I was wanting to ask you about, please.'

'Ask. Who is this?'

'It is Miss Nirmala Shahani.'

The lieutenant looked up sharply.

'Are you going to try and finger her for this?' he asked. 'You're not going home smelling of roses if you do.'

'No. No, I would not. But if it is the truth that she killed the Swami, then I would be very glad to prove it.'

'And you think it is? You think it may be after all?'

'I do not know,' Ghote answered soberly. 'But, Lieutenant, there are things I must ask her, and I must ask them in such circumstances that she will tell me more than she has told up to now.'

'What circumstances?'

The lieutenant's grey eyes were suddenly curious.

'I am wishing to question Miss Shahani at the scene of the crime, inside Swami's house.'

'I see.'

The lieutenant remained silent for what seemed a long time.

'No reason, so far as I can see,' he said at last, 'why I shouldn't tell the deputies guarding the place that my Bombay colleague can go have another look-see if he wants.'

'Thank you, Lieutenant.'

240

Ghote turned to go.

'Hoskins,' the lieutenant's cold voice came from behind him, 'if one little word of this gets out I personally will tear your licence into little pieces.'

'Yes, sir,' said Fred Hoskins.

But Ghote was unable to prevent the hulking private eye going with him to the Swami's fantastically-roofed house with Nirmala Shahani when he had found the girl in her hut and contrived to get her to accompany him without saying what their destination was.

When they had reached the central circle of the ashram and it had become clear they were heading for the Swami's house she had momentarily jibbed.

'Where—Where are we going?'

Ghote had put a firm hand to her elbow. He was determined to test her in the way he thought necessary. If really she had quarrelled with the Swami, had somehow come to snatch up his razor, had attacked him with it and had then spirited both the weapon and herself out of the big, bare room—But how? How?—then the best chance of breaking through the veneer of lies that she must have told him earlier lay in tackling her on the very spot where that bloody deed had been done.

Yet, looking down at her pretty face now, with that absurd, soft puppy nose, he found it hard to press on with what he knew he had to do.

If he had had a daughter . . .

'We are going into Swami's house. Do you mind that?'

Abruptly she straightened in his grasp.

'What is there to mind? I would be where Swamiji's spirit is.'

Nevertheless, inside, looking at the empty room with its blank wooden walls, its yellow-covered cushion throne, its white telephone, still dismembered after Lieutenant Foster's technicians' work on it, its close-fitting boarded floor with almost at the centre a dark-pink chalk outline and a rust-brown stain next to it, he was aware that the girl had shrunk deeply into herself.

He could feel it through the fingers of the hand that still grasped her elbow.

For one violent instant he wished that Fred Hoskins had not come into the lobby behind them. Alone with the girl he could have reassured her. Then, as violently, he was glad for once of the big private eye's hovering presence. Because the girl must not be reassured.

It could be—perhaps only just, but it could be—that she had lied to him before and had been lying again just a minute ago when she had said what she had about Swami's spirit.

And supposing what he guessed might have

happened had happened. Supposing there had been a quarrel, that the razor had been snatched up, that a wild sweeping blow had by chance been as effective as a slash deliberately inflicted by the man himself. Then, since she had not at once run out of the house weeping and screaming and shouting out for anybody there to hear about the terrible thing she had been unlucky enough to have done, then she must be prepared now still to lie. To lie and lie and lie again, and hope against hope that she would get away with it.

But, if that was the situation she was faced with, the strain on her—she was little more than a child after all—must be tremendous. A single jarring blow could snap her. Could snap her and reveal the truth. And provide an answer, an answer that must exist, to that absurd riddle of the vanished razor. That absurd and horribly demanding mystery.

Yet before he put his first question, before he delivered the jarring blow, he hesitated.

In the deepest part of his mind he did not expect that blow, however well delivered, was going to produce the answer. In the deepest part of his mind he was convinced that he already knew the answer and that it would not begin with a confession from Nirmala Shahani. It would begin with the fact that Swami had taken his own life. There, deep down, he knew this to be true, for all that, scrabble as he might, he

243

could not tease to the surface the next step in the train of logic that must lie there. The train that would end by his being able to explain, in terms that would satisfy the scientists of the Sheriff's Department, just what had happened.

CHAPTER SIXTEEN

Ghote, sure of his deep-down conviction that the Swami had committed suicide and had, by purely mechanical means, got rid of the razor he had used with the object of making a gesture which the world would be unable to ignore, hesitated to bang down in front of Nirmala Shahani's pretty, puppy-nose face a question brutal enough to break her if his belief was unfounded and she herself had killed the Swami.

But he knew that the logic of the situation, the logic of the four only who had known where the Swami was going to be at the time he had died, meant that the girl had to be tackled and tackled so toughly that she would come out with the truth whatever it was.

He hesitated. But he did no more than hesitate.

'Miss Shahani, when you came here, here to Swami's house, at midnight what was it that you quarrelled over?'

'No.'

The girl's illogical shout was a protest, a wild outflung protest.

Yet what exactly had she been protesting against? Was it against his flat assertion that she had come to the Swami when she had earlier told him she had not? Or was it against admitting to her mind once more a scene that must be appalling horrible to her?

'Come, it is no use to say no and no. That tale you were telling before, it was ridiculous only. Swami going to call you to him by putting the thought into your head. What nonsense. What nonsense only.'

'No. No, I tell you. No, He said that to me. He did. He made me that promise.'

'Miss Shahani, the time for lies is past. Swami could not have called you to him in that way. You know that.'

'No.'

But this protest was much, much less vigorous. There was a clear sound of strain underneath it. A hint of a whimper.

'Why deny and deny?' Ghote pressed in. 'Why go on like this? You know it is no use.'

'But he did say that to me. He could have called me by thought.'

He saw tears now in the big brown eyes on either side of that soft, absurd smudge of a nose. But tears were what he wanted to see. They were what he had to see if the girl was to break. And

245

if the answer to that mystery, the answer to where that vanished razor was, did after all lie with her, then she must be made to weep and to howl. And to confess.

'More nonsense. More utter rubbish only. That man could never have called you from your sleep by the power of his mind. You decided to go to him, isn't it? You wanted to come, and you pretended he had called. So you came.'

'No, no, no. I never came. He never called.'

'But you believed that he could? What happened when you found he could not?'

If she was not yet going to confess to murder, or if in fact she had nothing to confess, then, now that she was near desperation, perhaps he could wring from her at least an admission that the Swami was not all she had thought. Perhaps he could at least persuade her to come back to Bombay and her father.

Her breast was heaving under the loose-woven orange cotton of the shirt-like kameez she was wearing.

'I did believe he could call me,' she said. 'He could have called me. He did not last night. He had to go instead. To go from us all first. But he could have called me to him if he had wished.'

'Why do you believe and believe in that rogue? He could not have called. When did he ever call you before?'

He saw Nirmala's huge eyes full of despair.

'He had not done it before,' she answered in a

voice so low that he had to strain to catch the words close though they were standing to each other in the big, bare room. 'He always had to send someone for me. But that was my fault. My fault. I was not ready. I was not pure enough to hear.'

Less and less was it credible now that Nirmala had quarrelled here with the Swami, here on the bare boards of the floor under the bare wood of the high ceiling. But she had not yet been tested to the utmost. If she was a practised liar she could be lying still. Just. She could just be keeping herself above the swirling flood havoc he was seeking to thrust her down into. And a girl as young as this, as soft-nosed and appealing as a puppy, could yet be a practised liar.

And, damn it, once again he was deprived of the sight of tell-tale toes, this time by a pair of ugly, wooden-soled, slip-on clogs.

'Yes,' he jabbed on. 'You are not pure, Nirmala Shahani. There is blood on your hands. Isn't it? Isn't it? That blood.'

He pointed, suddenly and stiff-fingered, at the brownish stain not three yards away from them beside the dark-pink chalk outline that called back to his own mind vividly enough the body that had lain there, its luxuriant black locks outflung.

But Nirmala was slowly shaking her head in negative.

'No,' she said, more soberly now, 'that did

247

not happen. Swami was not killed by anybody but himself. The time had come for him to leave us, and he went.'

Ghote admitted defeat then.

There was not after all anything to break. He had tested the girl beyond any test that curled-up toes would have given an answer to, beyond any test that the electronic polygraph would have given an answer to. And she had come through unscathed.

He could not believe, as deep-down he had never believed, that she had indeed come to this building in the middle of the night, had quarrelled with the man she worshipped and had killed him. That razor-slash had not been a million-to-one lucky stroke from her hand. It had been a cut deliberately inflicted by the victim himself. That is what it had looked like when he had first seen it, and that was what it was. He was certain of that now.

Certain of it. And certain too that he was now, beyond dodging, face to face with the mystery of how the man who had cut his own throat had made the weapon that he had done it with disappear.

He raised his head to tell Nirmala Shahani that she could go. But then the thought of the task he had been sent here to California to carry out came back to him again.

'Miss Shahani,' he said, 'you may well be right that Swami took his own life. But you are not right when you say that that was anything but a coward's escape from a confidence trickster's self-made trap. He did not think the time had come for him to leave a wicked world. He was pressed by troubles and he took the easiest way out.'

'No.'

Nirmala was back to protesting now. The sound of her angry shout rang and echoed in the big, bare room.

'No,' she repeated, 'you are wrong, Inspector. Swamiji was a true great soul. I know it. I know it here.'

Her soft little fist thumped herself somewhere in the region of her heart.

Ghote was not greatly impressed. But she gave him no opportunity to point out that beliefs that were backed only by dim feelings somewhere inside needed to be confirmed by a few hard facts.

'No,' Nirmala tumbled on, all passion and trembling, 'Swamiji had to leave this dirty world with its dirty money-grubbing and its dirty lies. But when he went he left behind proof of what he was, of how a great soul can fly above everything in this world. He took away with his spirit the blade that ended his life.'

Ghote clamped his teeth hard together in vexation. He had no answer to that. Or, damn and blast it, he had the answer. Only it was somewhere locked deep in his own head.

Seemingly as little able to be confirmed by hard facts as was Nirmala's declaration that Swami was a great soul.

Nevertheless he was not going to let her think she had had the best of the encounter.

'Miss Shahani,' he said, 'I do not believe that Swami took away the razor with which he killed himself by any spiritual means. I know him to be a cheat only. He was cheating Mrs Russell Walters to get a Number One quality motor-car from her. He was bargaining with a person who wants to buy the ashram land just as if he was a Bombay housewife bargaining with a fisherwoman over a fat pomfret. He was perhaps also taking the worst advantage of girls who came here to the ashram believing in him. He could not have made that razor vanish by the power of his mind only.'

'Words,' said Nirmala. 'Words, words. Words only.'

Ghote looked at her solemnly.

'Yes,' he said, 'they are words only now. But I will prove them. Sooner or later I will prove them.'

It was as surprising to him as anything that he had met in surprising California when Nirmala, instead of turning away with a scornful if childish laugh, looked back at him as solemnly as he had looked at her.

'Inspector Ghote,' she said, 'if you can prove that that razor left this room in some ordinary

250

way, then I will know that, as you have said, Swami was not a great yogi. And if that is so, I will come back with you to my father as soon as a plane would take us.'

He stepped back a pace and looked at her, almost dazed.

So she did have doubts. She had doubts buried far inside her. She was not so absolutely sure about the Swami as she had claimed to be. She had some tiny niggling suspicion that the man might be a charlatan.

And, if she had that, then his own belief that the razor had not been spirited away, however little supported it was at present by fact, was suddenly all the nearer to being justified.

'Well, Miss Shahani,' he said, conscious that too long a silence had gone by, 'we would see. That is all. We would see.'

'You are no longer wanting me?' she asked, a docile girl once more.

'No, no. There is nothing more I am wanting to ask. Nothing.'

She left the bare, airy room straight away, not pausing to take even one last look round.

Was it because she was certain after all that she would have opportunities in plenty to come back here? When the place was a shrine visited daily by hundreds of disciples? Or was it because she could not bring herself to look at the place that was the very source of her secret doubts?

251

There was no telling.

But this was not the time to be wondering what a girl like Nirmala was or was not thinking. She was not the only one at the very source of doubts. Inspector Ganesh V. Ghote, of the Bombay CID (temporarily out of station) was also at the exact spot that enshrined the riddle he must find the answer to.

Or, rather, not so much find the answer to as reveal to himself the answer he was sure he had already found, lying where it was in that part of his mind which—blast it—there was no direct way down to.

He would just have to keep dropping random, hopeful fishing-lines into that deep, deep lake. And hope that one of them at last would entangle some thread and that bit by bit he would then be able to pull up a whole garment.

At least he was at the very place now where whatever had happened had occurred. That ought to be a help. If he could begin from this spot and slowly and carefully work things out.

'Gan boy, let me inform you I have been greatly interested to see an operative of the Bombay force at work in a hundred per cent interrogation situation.'

Fred Hoskins had been quiet, mercifully quiet, not even fully inside Swami's big, bare room but standing at the door of the lobby almost counterpoising giant-like the statue of the lively little Dancing Nataraj on its tall stand.

252

Evidently he was reluctant actually to set foot in a place where, according to his theory, Hindu magic had been performed.

If only the fellow had believed that influence was so strong that it would be risky to set foot in the building anywhere. But probably plain ordinary curiosity had worked on him too.

So now that little stretch of promised peace and quiet had been blown to pieces.

'It will have struck you however,' the intolerably loud voice hammered on, 'that the conclusion you have reached as a result of your interrogation was the one to which I myself had already come.'

'Yes, Fred,' Ghote said, 'what Miss Shahani told did bring me to an inevitable conclusion.'

It was not the conclusion Fred Hoskins had reached, which no doubt was the conclusion he had held on to with teeth clamped hard like a great overgrown bear ever since the beginning of the business, namely that Johnananda being somehow Hindu must be the mysterious murderer. But perhaps the fellow would not ask to have everything spelt out.

'Very well then, Gan, I am going to ask you a question.'

'Yes, Fred?'

'Gan, will you now accompany me to the office occupied by that man John—John—by that man Whatsit and use on him those techniques of interrogation which will produce a

253

confession of how he used his mystical powers to make the razor together with his own body transport itself from the scene to a place of safety?'

'No, Fred, I will not.'

Ghote contrived to state his refusal so firmly that for once Fred Hoskins heard what had been said.

'Whaddya mean—no?'

Ghote straightened his bonily thin shoulders.

'I mean that I do not intend to question Johnananda,' he said. 'I do not believe he is the type of man to kill in cold blood for gain, and even if I did I do not believe that, whatever orange garments he wraps himself up in, he is capable of performing the feat of bi-location.'

'Bi-loca what?'

'Bi-location. It is the feat of removing the body in an instant of time from one place to another. It is well known to take place in India. But it is not, I repeat not, something that that Englishman could ever perform. And for that reason I have no intention whatsoever of going to him and accusing.'

He watched fascinated as into Fred Hoskins's beef-red face so much extra blood came thundering up that within moments it took on the dark purplish hue of meat too long exposed to the air.

It was several seconds before words came to relieve the pressure. But when they came they arrived in torrents.

'The hell you're not. Now listen to me. It's plain that that guy killed the Swami. He killed him for one very simple reason. So as to take over. He could see what a sweet racket the Swami was on to, and he wanted in. Anyone would have. It's as simple as that. I'm telling you, Gan, that guy is the killer, and the only thing still to find out is just how he used these Hindu methods to commit his crime. Now that is a subject on which you, as a Hindu and a police officer, are in a position to catch him out. And you are going to do it. You're my boy, Inspector Goat, and you're the one who's going to crack this case wide open.'

Ghote took breath to say no again. But the mere look on his face was evidently enough for the enormous private eye.

'And if you're not going to do your plain duty, Inspector, then, by God, Fred Hoskins is going to do it for you. Maybe I don't have your understanding of Hindu tricks, but I know how to make a witness talk when he's holding back on me and I'm going to do that right now.'

Fury swooshed into Ghote's head.

'You will not,' he said. 'You will keep out of this, Mr Hoskins.'

'Just you try and stop me.'

And Fred Hoskins, grain-sack belly whirling, swung round and charged out of the flapping double doors of the house.

255

CHAPTER SEVENTEEN

Ghote, with one brief despairing hankering for the spell of quiet thought he had been about to have, set off at a run after the hulking private eye. He was not far behind by the time the fellow entered the administration building and a moment later he heard that motor-horn voice demanding from anybody who could hear—and nobody could have failed to do that—where John—Johnwhatsit was.

As in his turn he ran up the steps into the building he became aware of a change in the atmosphere there. The deputy on duty in the central corridor was no longer standing smartly upright. He was instead slouched against the wall. And the door of the office Lieutenant Foster had taken over had not opened swiftly at the sound of the rumpus outside.

'The lieutenant?' he asked sharply. 'Where is he?'

'Gone down the hill to get himself a bite to eat,' the deputy replied.

Then from an office further along Ghote heard Fred Hoskins's bellow again.

'Meditating? Meditating? And where the hell's Look-out Point?'

The answer was inaudible, but it must have included directions because the next moment

256

there came the crash of a door and Fred Hoskins came thundering down the corridor.

Ghote considered for an instant interposing his own slight frame between the fellow and his way out. But, though he reckoned he would be able to stop him, he doubted if he would succeed in detaining him for any length of time by argument or reasoning.

Better to follow and try to intervene when he had found Johnananda.

But, trotting after the enormous private eye through the dusk back across the inner circle of the ashram, Ghote found he had made a miscalculation. Ahead of him, Fred Hoskins had gone for his wide, green monster of a car, slammed into its driving seat and shot off into the dark.

Ghote came to a halt and cursed.

How could he follow now? And what damage would the fellow have done before he managed to secure transport and catch up with him?

Then, in the last of the light, his eye caught a glimpse of the old bicycle that still rested in the passageway between Swami's house and the dining-hall. Shooting down the hill on that, he might not be so far behind.

He set off again at a run.

But before he had even reached the ancient machine he remembered in what a state of disrepair it had been when he had last noticed it, and when he got to it he found it in no better

257

condition. The front wheel still had its tyre dangling loosely round the metal rim and there was no sign as far as he could see even of the orange inner-tube.

But then he noticed in which direction Fred Hoskins's monster car—its headlamps were blazing out now—had gone.

It was not heading down the hill towards the Visitors Centre and the whole of California spread out in its network of mighty roads beyond but up towards the tree-covered ridge above the ashram. Look-out Point, of course that must be at the crest of the ridge somewhere. And that should not be so far away.

He began to run again, setting himself now a steady pace that he hoped to keep up all the way to the top of the ridge. But even running it took him a full ten minutes, peering into the deeper darkness under the great unsweeping redwoods, to reach the crest.

Before he quite got there, however, he saw Fred Hoskins's car. It seemed to have been pulled off the dirt track and was pointing along the ridge to the left. Its headlights were still blazing out, so much stronger and more fiercely white than the lamps of the Fiats and Ambassadors of night-time Bombay.

He got to the car, panting like a dog, and saw that it was empty, the driver's door swung fully open.

Where had that madman gone?

Then over the sound of his own puffing he caught a distant, familiar noise. A yammer-yammer-yammering.

It was coming from the direction the big green car's headlights were pointing in, and he set out once more, running again and on the soft reddish earth silent.

The yammering grew moment by moment louder.

Oddly, in these alien surroundings, there came into his head as he pushed himself towards the sound, a fleeting memory of his own earliest childhood. The village. The reedy pond at its edge where boys less high in the scale than the schoolmaster's son took the buffaloes to wallow. And the noise of the small flotilla of ducks that made the muddy pond their home. A never-ending, honking quacking.

But to hell with childhood memories. What was that man doing to Johnananda?

Now he could begin to make out the words.

'...take it just once more ... that you plotted and planned... Don't tell me the ashram isn't a classy operation... I tell you that you were eaten up with envy for the man they call the Swami With No Name, and I further—'

'Fred.'

Ghote shouted as loudly as his panting breath would let him.

By the faint light still coming from those

powerful headlamps behind him he had been able to make out in front of the hugely tall private eye the orange-clad form of Johnananda. He was kneeling, actually kneeling, on the hard surface of a big all-but-buried rock, a picture of abjectness.

And Fred Hoskins was holding his gun on him.

Ghote staggered up over the last few paces that separated them.

'Fred,' he said. 'Fred.'

'Ah, it's you, Gan boy. It'll be a pleasure for you to witness the final confirmation of your theories on the case. The man I have in front of me, by name John-something-or-other, is spilling, Gan.'

'Spilling?' Ghote puffed out. 'You mean he is confessing?'

He drew in a deep, painful breath.

'Fred,' he said, 'you have been with him for a good time, for ten minutes at least, isn't it?'

The immense private eye gave a swift glance at the watch on his wrist, still keeping his gun menacingly pointed at the kneeling form of Johnananda in front of him.

'Yes, Gan, as a former officer of the LAPD I naturally consulted my wristwatch at the moment of apprehending the alleged perpetrator now before me.'

'Yes, Fred. And you have been asking questions for all that time then. So, tell me,

260

please, how did he get himself and that razor out of Swami's house? Has he told you that?'

'In the course of my interrogation,' Fred Hoskins answered, 'the suspect has acknowledged he was the legal heir and successor to the deceased.'

'But, damn it, has he told you how he got out of that house when myself and two deputies also were watching the only possible exit?'

Peering towards Johnananda, as if perhaps he would provide the answer which the belly-jutting private eye was so stubbornly not giving, Ghote thought that in the dim light of the distant powerful headlights he could detect on those fleshless, sunken cheeks gleaming streaks that could only be tears.

Fred Hoskins, the gun in his huge fist pointing directly at Johnananda's head still, continued to remain silent.

'Has he told you how?' Ghote repeated stormily. 'Has he? Has he?'

'The suspect has admitted his crime.'

Fred Hoskins's uncompromising statement, for all that it failed to give the answer to the tormenting riddle of Swami's house, brought home thumpingly to Ghote just what that claim about 'spilling' had really meant. It had meant that the huge incubus had been right all along. It meant that his own judgement of Johnananda must have been totally wrong. It meant that Hoskins had triumphed.

261

'He has told you that he killed Swami?' he blurted out, unable to provide any more logical response to the private eye's assertion.

Fred Hoskins, gun unwavering, repeated exactly the words he had used before.

'The suspect has fully admitted his crime. I suggest you pay attention, Inspector. There has been a full confession, and it now only remains for me to escort the suspect to the proper authorities, namely Lieutenant Foster of the Los Angeles County Sheriff's Department, for him there to repeat his statement.'

'But Lieutenant Foster is not at the ashram.'

It was the best Ghote could find to say.

'Then it will be your duty to guard the prisoner while I take him to the Hall of Justice in LA.'

'But the lieutenant has gone to get something to eat only,' Ghote found himself saying. 'He would be back in a short time.'

He felt a bubbling fury with himself that he had somehow got involved in absurd argument over a pure incidental.

'In that case,' Fred Hoskins yammered in answer, 'I will hand over to you, Inspector, my piece, since you are unfortunate enough not to be packing, and we'll escort the prisoner back to the ashram where I will requisition some place of safety where he may be kept locked up until such time as the lieutenant return.'

Oh, why can't he stop, Ghote thought.

And at the same time he heard his own voice, inanely, continuing the ridiculous discussion.

'I do not think, Fred, there is such a place of safety in the ashram. You may not have observed it, but they do not anywhere use locks.'

'That fact has naturally come under my observation,' the huge private eye went relentlessly on. 'I will however take the necessary steps to locate a place in the ashram where some standards of security exist.'

Liar, thought Ghote. You observed nothing, and you can think of nowhere down there safe enough.

And, all the while that the pointless wrangling had been going on, he had been aware that the man it concerned was kneeling beside them on the rocky ground, menaced by a gun, his face wet with tears.

He wanted to turn aside, go over to him, put a hand on his shoulder and offer a word of reassurance. But the sheer baldness of Fred Hoskins's claim stopped him. The fellow had said that Johnananda had confessed to killing the Swami. It could not have been stated more clearly. And if that was so, then it would be quite wrong for him to offer any comfort.

Then, suddenly, a thought made itself apparent in his head. A wicked, malicious thought. And an irresistible one.

'Fred,' he said, 'there is one building at the
263

ashram that is altogether secure although it has no lock.'

'Good man,' the private eye boomed out. 'I knew I could rely on you. Where do we take him?'

'To Swami's house,' Ghote replied.

'But—But—'

Fred Hoskins turned right away from Johnananda. His gun was pointing now, if anywhere, at Ghote's right foot.

'But,' Ghote said, 'you were going to ask, what if he uses his magical power to get out of there just as he must have used it after he had killed Swami.'

'Yeah. Well, hell, Gan...'

Ghote played his trump card then.

'If he does that, Fred,' he said, 'you would have proved and proved that you were right all along concerning the identity of the culprit.'

Would the fellow rise to the bait? Perhaps it had better be dangled yet more obviously. After all, if there was any doubt about the confession he had claimed to have extracted, then if Johnananda could be protected from the threat of that gun perhaps the truth would eventually come out.

'You would be proved right, Fred,' he said persuasively. 'And the rest of us would be proved wrong.'

'Gan boy, I think you've come up with the answer. We'll incarcerate this guy in the

264

Swami's house and we'll maintain a strict guard over the sole means of exit.'

'First-class idea,' Ghote said.

★   ★   ★

They escorted Johnananda to the Swami's house in silence. Ghote sat with their prisoner in the back of the big car, holding Fred Hoskins's gun discreetly by his side. Only as they were marching up the steps into the building did he venture to put to Johnananda the question that he had obtusely wanted to ask him directly himself ever since Fred Hoskins had announced that confession. Up till now he had felt he could hardly put it to Johnananda under the private eye's very nose, but at this last moment sheer curiosity made him throw tact to the winds.

'Johnananda,' he said rapidly, 'is it right that you took Swami's life?'

But without a moment of hesitation the Englishman answered in a tear-croaky voice.

'Yes, I killed him.'

Ghote did not dare ask for details. The three words had at once in any case deprived him of determination. *I killed him.* They had turned upside down in an instant his own old, laboriously-arrived-at belief that the Swami's death was suicide not murder. They had questioned to the core the obstinate notion he had cherished that there was a simple answer to

265

the mystery of the missing razor and that that answer, complete in all its details, lay somewhere in the depths of his mind.

'Gan boy, I am going to ask you something.'

Oh hell.

'Yes, Fred?'

'Gan, I am going to entrust to you the task of checking and double-checking on the interior of this building. I, in the meanwhile, will hold the prisoner at gunpoint. It will be your duty to ascertain that the conditions of security pertaining here at the time of the killing still pertain in their entirety.'

'Yes, Fred. You can rely on me for that.'

So he went into that big, bare room again ahead of Johnananda, switching on the lights that showed every square inch of those blank surfaces, Fred Hoskins, gun in his huge fist again, waited in the little lobby with his prisoner and the statue of the Dancing Nataraj, the lifeless one all life, the alive one almost as if dead.

He marched round the big room, though he knew there was nothing to see in it that had not been examined a hundred times. He kicked and prodded again at the yellow-covered cushion-throne. He stared down at the white dismembered telephone. He went into the bathroom at the far end, and noted once again that it did not contain a cut-throat razor and that there was no possible means of egress from it.

He went into the little bedroom next door and once again looked at the solitary, well-sprung bed with the drawers under it that had been searched and searched again. He even riffled through the pile of bright car brochures, pulled one out and attempted to read a few words of it. Only the pages were so glossy that in the bright light that proved impossible.

No, there was still no way that he could see how anyone could have got out of the place in the time between the instant the Swami's blood had begun to pour from his slashed throat and that moment, not ten minutes later, when he himself had seen the still liquid scarlet.

He went back to the lobby where Fred Hoskins and Johnananda were waiting.

'Checked, Fred,' he said at his most clipped.

'Okay then, bud,' the towering private eye said to Johnananda. 'You cool your sweet heels in there for a while, and then you can have the pleasure of repeating to Lieutenant Foster just what you said to me.'

Johnananda walked, head hanging, into the big room. Ghote shut its door on him, followed Fred Hoskins out into the night and then pulled the double doors of the house closed behind them.

'Gan,' boomed Fred Hoskins, 'I will now inform you of my immediate intentions.'

Does he have to, Ghote thought, feeling battered and yet more battered.

267

'Yes, Fred?'

'Now, Gan boy, you are going to get us some food. It may have escaped your attention, my friend, but you and I have not renewed the inner man for a good many hours.'

'No, Fred, you are right. We have not.'

It was true that it was a long time since they had eaten an early lunch at the motel, though he himself did not feel as if he could swallow a single mouthful of anything. The whole underlying force that had kept him going throughout the entire, dismaying affair, the belief that the Swami's death must have some rational explanation, seemed to be tumbled into ruins. Nothing mattered now.

But, obediently, he crossed the circle, lit only by the light coming through windows here and there, and presented himself at the kitchens to beg a share in the ashram's evening meal for himself as well as the private eye. No point in going back with only one plate. The hectoring questions which that would bring down on him did not bear thinking of.

The disciples clearing up in the kitchens were smilingly delighted to provide him with food. A girl with a tiny squabby baby papoose-like on her back scurried off to find him a tray, a bright orange plastic one. A boy with a long swatch of hair held in place by a rubber-band, also orange, spread disposable paper plates on it while Ghote wondered why they did not use convenient

268

broad leaves for the purpose. A particularly skinny-looking younger girl wearing a T-shirt inscribed *I Love Swami* and a boy who had plainly attempted, though without success, to grow luxuriant curls like his dead guru's began heaping out food left over from the meal.

It was, Ghote noticed, much the same type of food that might be served in an ashram in India, lentils, beans, tomatoes, rice. But it was much, much more abundant and somehow, too, each bean, each grain of lentil, seemed to be bigger and glossier than it would have been at home.

'This is far tastier than anything grown with chemicals,' the boy with the impoverished curls assured him, ladling out another spoonful.

'Yeah, and much better for you,' said the girl with the baby on her back.

'Thank you, thank you,' he said, picking up the tray and hurrying out.

No doubt Fred Hoskins was guarding the doors of Swami's house as rigorously as could be imagined. And yet . . . And yet . . .

But across on the other side of the half-darkened circle, he found the huge private eye sitting on the steps of Swami's house, gun in hand, looking fully content with his lot.

'All is well?' he asked him.

'Couldn't be better.'

He laid the tray from the kitchens on the step.

Fred Hoskins peered at it in the poor light.

'What the heck is this? You didn't order

269

steak.'

'They are not eating any sort of meat in the ashram.'

He saw that huge belly swell in the gloom.

'No meat? No wonder those jerks are incapable of rational behaviour. Let me inform you, Gan, it's an American's right to eat good red meat daily.'

'Yes, Fred.'

Ghote saw again the enormous, lolloping steak, oozing red blood that he had watched the belly-jutting private eye consume on the first occasion they had eaten together. Was it this right to bloody meat that Americans possessed that was the cause of all the violence in the land?

He settled down on the step on the other side of the vegetarian tray.

No, he thought, we in India can be very, very violent also.

Fred Hoskins picked up one of the plates and a spoon.

'There's no ice-cream,' he exploded, apparently just realizing the outrage. 'Ice-cream, Gan boy, is essential in every red-blooded American's diet.'

'Yes. Is it? That is most interesting, Fred.'

He found that with the aroma of the food in his nostrils he was after all hungry. He ate voraciously—the various dishes were excellent, though not very spicy—and even polished off two of the plates that Fred Hoskins had disdained in favour of recounting other items that were necessary to all red-blooded Americans and then branching off into tales of how a certain extremely red-blooded American had shown his red-bloodedness to best advantage patrolling the streets of Los Angeles.

Eating some of this *dal* would be much better for him, Ghote thought, trying to deny admittance to the stream of yammering, hammering, honking, quacking verbiage.

At last underneath the continuing din—'You are going to thank me for this, Gan boy. I am about to tell you how I took one Pete Benito, wanted for Grand Theft Auto, when he...'— he thought he detected the sound of a car labouring up the dirt-track hill. Then he caught a glimpse of headlights and in a few moments Lieutenant Foster's vehicle pulled up just outside the circle.

'Fred,' he interrupted, 'the lieutenant has come.'

Fred Hoskins surged to his feet.

'This will be a memorable experience for you, Gan,' he said. 'You are about to witness your first arrest on American soil.'

'Yes, Fred.'

He let the big private eye do the talking, while he stood keeping those double-doors under unremitting observation. It meant that the explanations took a good deal longer than if he had been able to put his quiet, unsmiling

271

colleague from the Sheriff's Department in the picture himself, but he was determined not to be associated, however remotely, with the idea of Johnananda as the Swami's murderer. Not because, after those three words of confession on the steps of Swami's house, he could any longer pretend that there was any other explanation of the business, but because he could not bring himself to acknowledge out aloud that after all some mystic means must have been used in the killing, and used too by a person he himself had dismissed as a mere play-acting Englishman.

Yet Emily, he remembered now with shame, had even said clearly that Johnananda possessed powers that people in the West could not attain. And Fred Hoskins had drawn his attention to her words.

Lieutenant Foster heard out the private eye's long, self-regarding account, delivered through his car window, in silence. He did not even offer a comment until he had opened the car door, got out and taken a quick, assessing survey of the whole area round.

Then he turned to Ghote.

'Inspector?'

Ghote felt the single questioning word as if it had been a punch to the solar plexus, perfectly timed. He was not going to be allowed to escape endorsing Fred Hoskins's statement.

He pulled back his shoulders.

'As we put Johnananda into Swami's house,' he answered, 'he uttered three words to me. He said: I killed him.'

'Yup.'

Without another word the lieutenant headed across to the Swami's house. Ghote followed close at his heels. Behind him, a huge triumphant shadow, he felt rather than saw Fred Hoskins.

The lieutenant mounted the steps of the house, pushed open the outer doors, crossed the Nataraj-protected lobby, pushed open the inner door and entered the big, bare room where the Swami had died.

Johnananda was not there.

CHAPTER EIGHTEEN

The doors of the two small rooms at the rear of Swami's house were open, as Ghote himself had left them after completing his examination of the place before they had put Johnananda into it. It had been possible from where the three of them stood by the entrance to see right into the bathroom and bedroom. But Lieutenant Foster, after giving Ghote just the briefest of questioning glances, strode across the big, close-boarded, empty main room and stepped into each in turn.

Eventually he came out of the bedroom and stood by its door, his tanned face more expressionless than Ghote had yet seen it.

Ghote felt a huge interior desolation. He had said to Fred Hoskins, by way of secretly paying him out for many hours of quacking boredom, that if Johnananda were to disappear from this solid, escape-proof building then it would finally nail the case against the man. But he had not for one moment expected such a thing to happen.

And now it had. Johnananda had done precisely what he himself had firmly believed was impossible for a person of his standing.

'Well,' he said into the air. 'He has done it. He has done it for the second time.'

'Where'll he be, Inspector?' Lieutenant Foster said.

Ghote lifted pained eyes to the wooden ceiling above.

'Since he has gone from here,' he answered, 'he could be anywhere. In India even. In Tibet. In his office over in the administration block. Anywhere.'

'I guess so.'

They stood in silence. Even Fred Hoskins had been reduced to speechlessness by the spectacular proof of his own theory.

'Should I put out an all-stations call?' the lieutenant asked at last, plainly afraid he was making a fool of himself by the suggestion.

274

'Oh, yes,' Ghote replied. 'Why not? After all, he may just have moved himself to somewhere nearby where one of your deputies would see him. He could be in California still.'

In California, he thought. Someone, a murderer when all was said and done, who had transported himself by the process of bi-location from one part of California to another. Of California.

'I'll have to get to a phone that works,' Lieutenant Foster said, moving towards the door with a semblance of his old decisiveness.

Ghote followed him out of the house and over to the administration block. They mounted its steps.

And, as they did so, Ghote caught the faint sound of a raised voice coming from somewhere along the central corridor. A raised, high-pitched, familiar voice.

'. . . very kind. Very kind of you, Mr Lansing. Then we'll say next Thursday at eleven o'clock. Sorry not to make it earlier, but one is snowed under, but snowed under.'

He went at a belting run along the corridor. He heard the tink of a telephone receiver being put down. He glanced swiftly over his shoulder. The lieutenant, who had paused bewildered for an instant, was hurrying after him now. He flung open the door of Johnanandas office without ceremony.

The sunken-cheeked, shaven-headed

275

Englishman was sitting at his papers-covered, orange plastic desk.

For three long seconds Ghote looked at him. He needed that much time to convince himself that he was seeing what he was seeing.

Lieutenant Foster had come up beside him and was standing equally silent. Ghote spared a moment to glance back to see what Fred Hoskins was doing. The mountainous private eye was still at the entrance to the building, a hey-you-guys expression plastered all across his great beef-red face.

Ghote turned back to Johnananda. And, as he did so, he knew what he had to ask him.

'Johnanandaji,' he said, choosing the honorific form of his name with deliberation. 'Johnanandaji, if you are the yogi you have just shown yourself to be, far along the path, you did not kill Swami. Please, then, why did you say that you had?'

Johnananda looked back at him. He had shown no surprise when his door had been so abruptly flung open, nor when first Ghote and then Lieutenant Foster had stood there looking in at him without uttering a word between them. Now he gave them a smile, a rather worn smile.

'But I did kill Swami,' he said. 'It was my fault he took his own life. My fault, if ever anything was.'

'Yes,' Ghote answered, 'I know now that

276

Swami did, of course, take his own life. It was only when you seemed to say very, very clearly that you had killed him that I made the mistake of believing that you had actually cut his throat with that razor.'

'No, no.'

'No, I know. But, tell me please, what exactly do you mean when you say it was your fault he took his life?'

'But, my dear chap, poor Swami was such a cheat, such a cheat towards the end. And at last everything caught up with him. But, you see, I had been letting him go on, and when he killed himself I saw that that had been a terrible mistake.'

'Yes, I see. But why, please, did you let him go on like that, cheating and cheating? I do not understand.'

Johnananda gave them his pale smile again.

'Well, when he came out here to California first he was a truly God-realized person. A true yogi. But, you know, one of the great Masters once said that everything on this earth is like a mingling of sand and sugar. Be like the wise and, he said, take only the sugar. But, poor Swami, after a while he began to think that Californian sand was sweeter than sugar.'

'And you knew this? You saw it?'

'Well, one doesn't like to boast about one's own spiritual stature, but one can see what one can see. And it wasn't difficult to see Swami had lost his spiritual voltage if one was lucky enough to have eyes. Not your sort of seeing eyes, I'm afraid, Inspector and Lieutenant. But my sort. Our sort here.'

'Yes,' said Ghote.

Johnananda's fleshless face took on a brief look of pain.

'You see, to begin with Swami wasn't doing any real harm,' he said. 'I thought I could keep an eye on the boys and girls and see that his loss of voltage didn't affect them. And it didn't for a long time, you know. I mean, until shortly before the end he wasn't making hay with any of them sexually or anything.'

'But finally he was,' Ghote said. 'Finally he was ravishing those young girls, isn't it? And you told me that he was not.'

Johnananda's long-fingered hands flapped once like a pair of exhausted fishes.

'Well, my dear, I didn't tell you that, not plainly,' he said. 'It was wrong of me, I know, even to try to mislead you, picking and choosing all those double-meaning phrases. But Swami was dead then and I thought it wouldn't matter if I tried to preserve the memory of him as a remarkable man. He was, you know. When he came West, he was remarkable. He had a great deal to give.'

He looked at them both as they stood in the doorway, his judges.

'Okay,' Lieutenant Foster said. 'I'm prepared

278

to accept that on your say-so. Now.'

'Hey!'

A clamorous bellow came from just behind them. Fred Hoskins had arrived. He was staring at Johnananda over their shoulder as if he was simultaneously confronting both a huge, red-blooded American steak and a genuine, clanking, head-under-arm, white-sheeted, mopping and mowing ghost.

'So,' he broke into yammering speech, 'you didn't make it, eh, bud? You couldn't get yourself far enough away. Well, I've got news for you. The Californian police aren't so easy to fool. You've cooked your goose now, boy. You've just given us the final proof of the method you used to murder that innocent man. We've outwitted you at every point. I now notify you that you thought you had us fooled when we put you into that Swami house just now, but, no sir, we now have proof that we...'

Mr Quack.

Mr Quack, Mr Quack, Mr Quack, Ghote thought. How much longer are you going to go on quack-quack-quacking? But I do not care. That's all your noise means to me now. A duck on a pond, quacking and quacking.

Carry on. Carry on as long as you want. I have got a little quiet thinking to do, and your quack-quacking will not put me off one little bit.

The honking private eye may have gone on

with his diatribe a little longer. Ghote did not hear him. What brought him at last out of his inward-turned, jumping from point to point reverie was Lieutenant Foster's quiet voice.

'That'll do, Hoskins. We'll leave Mr Johnananda now.'

'Yes,' Ghote said. 'Yes, Lieutenant, please let us leave. There is something I am very much wanting to show you.'

'Yes, Inspector?'

'I am wanting to show you, Lieutenant, where is that razor now.'

A little smile lifted the corners of the lieutenant's mouth.

'You are?'

'Yes, please. Please, come. It would be best, it would be easiest if we go back to Swami's house.'

'Okay.'

The two of them walked, not hurrying, not dawdling, back across the ashram's central circle in the direction of the familiar, spiral-roofed building. Fred Hoskins, Ghote was just aware, was following them puzzledly. But he no longer bothered about the fellow.

Fred Hoskins was exorcized at last. Yammering giant had been transmogrified into Mr Quack, the duck on the pond.

'So he committed suicide after all,' the lieutenant said thoughtfully. 'Whatever he may have been once, when it came to the end he was

280

no more than a plain con-man, using his hold on those girls for his own enjoyment. And then all of a sudden things got too tough for him. He knew he wouldn't be able to get out of what I'd got on him, and he must have reckoned that a guy as noticeable as he was wouldn't have lasted a week if he'd tried to run for it. So it was goodbye everybody.'

He darted a sharp glance at Ghote.

'And you're going to tell me how he pulled off that last trick?' he said.

'Yes,' Ghote said, unemphatically, 'I am going to do that. You know, in the end the fellow was no more than what in India we are calling a bhaghat, a conjuror fellow.'

'Okay.'

Instead of leading the lieutenant to the Swami's house, however, he took him to the entrance to the passageway between the house and the dining-hall.

'Before we go in,' he said, 'I would like you to see something here.'

'I'm interested.'

Ghote pointed.

'It is that bicycle, Lieutenant,' he said. 'You can make it out by the light from the dining-hall windows. I saw it myself when I first came to the ashram. I noticed that somebody had begun to repair it and then had stopped. To tell you the truth, it reminded me of India because of that, and I was somewhat pleased. And all the time I have been here I thought that I was remembering the machine because of that only.'

'But?' said the lieutenant.

'But what I was not realizing until just now, when for the first time I seemed to have quiet so as to be able to think, was that when I first saw the bicycle before the Swami took his life the wheel under repair had its inner-tube lying loose with it. But when I looked at the machine again after the Swami's death that inner-tube was missing.'

'A rubber inner-tube,' the lieutenant said pensively. 'Go on, Inspector.'

'Well now, please, I would like you to step into the Swami's house.'

'Okay.'

They entered the lobby of the house. But Ghote stopped before opening the inner door.

'Please look at this little statue,' he said. 'It is of a god we are calling Nataraj. He is dancing the creation and destruction of the universe. But his statue here is small, and so it has been put on this tall pillar.'

Lieutenant Foster stood looking at the Dancing Nataraj and the solid pillar it stood on.

'You could, if you lifted the statue off and were agile enough, climb on to that pillar,' he said.

'Yes,' Ghote said. 'Shall we take it inside?'

'I'll bring it. You go ahead.'

Ghote went into the Swami's big, bare room

once more and walked over the close-fitted boards until he came to the dark-pink outline that the lieutenant's technicians had marked out. The lieutenant came up a moment later, hugging the heavy pillar to his chest.

'Put it just here,' Ghote said.

The lieutenant placed it as he had been asked.

'Perhaps you could help me to get up on it,' Ghote said. 'I would be able to do it on my own, but it would be quicker with some help.'

'Sure.'

The lieutenant put his arms round the pillar to steady it and thrust out a knee so that Ghote could step up. In a moment he was perched high, looking not at all like the elegant little statue in the lobby.

'Yes,' he said. 'You can see I can reach this tall ceiling now.'

'Yup. I see.'

'And this, I suppose, will be the one.'

'Guess so.'

Ghote placed both hands flat on the wooden ceiling panel immediately above his head. As his fingers touched it a momentary doubt flickered through him. But it was momentary only.

He pushed vigorously upwards and the panel, hinged on one side, flopped back open. He put his hands through the black square that was revealed and, straining up on tiptoe, stretched till he could get his elbows on to the sides of the surrounding frame. Then with one wriggling heave he hauled himself right up.

As soon as he had recovered his breath he began calling down his findings.

'Yes, the inner-tube is here.'

'Fine.'

'It is fastened with drawing-pins on each side.'

'Known as thumb-tacks in this part of the world. But I get the picture. The inner-tube makes a sort of big catapult, right?'

'Right. And still tied to the middle of it there is the razor. I am taking care not to touch.'

'Okay. Anything else?'

'Yes. I think there was also a length of cotton, orange cotton, that held back the trap-door until the inner-tube came right through and broke it.'

'Guess there would have to be something like that. Well, that just about wraps it up then. Nice straightforward case. Right?'

'Right, Lieutenant.'

CHAPTER NINETEEN

It was very different from Los Angeles. Lanes so narrow that the relentless sun could not penetrate their depths were filled thick with people. People jabbering, gesticulating, sleeping, chanting, arguing, standing, lying, squatting, bargaining, lost in prayer. Pilgrims, tourists, naked sadhus striding out brandishing their iron tridents, beggars, white-clad widows with stark shaven heads, white-skinned hippies wandering drug-bemused, pundits inexhaustibly expounding, touts busy and pouncing 'Just take my card only, no obligation to buy.' Cows, slow, bony and arrogant, moved here and there through them all. Dogs scavenged, scratched, slept, fought. Goats strained at ropes, nibbled, butted. Flights of brilliant green parrots darted.

It was pulsatingly noisy. Pipes moaned and screeched. Drums thrummed and boomed. Transistor radios poured out music, film music, holy music. Temple bells clanked almost continuously as worshippers entered and brought their presence to the attention of the god within. Car-horns honked and bleated. Bicycle-bells jangled.

And everything was directed down towards the mighty, slow-drifting river, Holy Ganges, with its great, stone-stepped ghats alive with pilgrims and beggars and holy men and holy-seeming rogues and simple bathers and yet simpler washers of clothes. Motor-coaches poured out their passengers here. A big yellow tourist vehicle spewed a whole load of camera-toting Americans. Guides seized on them. Priests beside the funeral pyres bickered formidably over the price of the necessary supply of sandalwood and verse by verse over the necessary Sanskrit readings.

Protima, her long-cherished ambition realized at last, and only some ten days later than she had originally hoped for, was in her element. Little Ved beside her was wide-eyed with wonder.

Ghote was less pleased. But he was there, in holy Banaras, a pilgrim like the thousands upon thousands of others.

They crossed the great greenish river to the far sandy side where in a wide open space the saint whom Protima had particularly wished to hear was addressing an enormous crowd, patient under the broiling sun. Baba, wearing white homespun of a dazzling purity, sat cross-legged on his high, awning-covered pandal sending his words spilling out in gentle waves over the thousands in front of him.

From the angle at which Ghote at last found himself looking, the old man's sweetly-bearded visage was obscured by the fat ball of the microphone that dangled from its boom in front of him. But Ghote was not worried by that. Instead, he contented himself with letting his eyes roam over the crowd all round.

And it was then that he spotted a face at once sharply familiar and, for a moment, unplaceable. Where was it he had seen that particular girl before?

Ridiculous. The face was as well-known to him surely as—as his own son's.

Then the girl turned her head a little and he caught her in full profile. At once he recognized, seen close-to in Bombay less than a week before, a soft smudgy little nose, a countenance that was a new-born puppy's or a deer's, inquisitive, innocent, fearfully in danger from the harshnesses of the world.

Nirmala Shahani, it seemed, had found herself a new guru.

T

Chivers Large Print Direct

If you have enjoyed this Large Print book and would like to build up your own collection of Large Print books and have them delivered direct to your door, please contact **Chivers Large Print Direct**.

Chivers Large Print Direct offers you a full service:

☆ **Created to support your local library**

☆ **Delivery direct to your door**

☆ **Easy-to-read type and attractively bound**

☆ **The very best authors**

☆ **Special low prices**

For further details either call Customer Services on 01225 443400 or write to us at

Chivers Large Print Direct
FREEPOST (BA 1686/1)
Bath
BA1 3QZ